ROOT OF ALL EVIL

LIBBY HOWARD

CHAPTER 1

"I'm not getting into the dumpster." I fixed my boss, J.T. Pierson, with a stern look.

"Uh, me either. So don't even think about asking." Daisy wrinkled her nose and took a sidestep away from the metal container.

We were in the narrow street behind the parking deck where Luanne Trainor had breathed her last. The case had brought almost as much media attention to Milford as Holt Dupree's death had to Locust Point, and my boss was determined to capitalize on the event by filming an episode on the murder for his YouTube channel. There'd already been a few snags in this production. Detective Keeler had not only refused to perform in the reenactment, he'd refused to be interviewed at all. That left me to be the star of the show.

I'd repeatedly told J.T. I was done acting in his low-budget reality show. There were only so many hours in the day. At work, my focus was on our actual work, and once I was off the clock, I really didn't want to be an amateur actress in J.T.'s obsessive hobby. He'd managed to talk me into this one in a moment of weakness, when I was excited over receiving my investigator's license. So far, beyond the interview I'd only had to appear with Daisy and some extras J.T. had grabbed off the street for the meet-and-greet scene, and walk through the parking garage to gasp in shock over the spot where Luanne had lain. That hadn't been easy because the shadowy figure of her ghost was still hanging around the spot where she'd died, recreating the event over and over again in a weird loop that only I could see. I'd managed to get through that section of J.T.'s video in one take, walking through the icy chill of Luanne's spirit to head to the sunny, narrow road behind the parking garage and businesses along the main street.

That had been bad enough. I was drawing the line at the dumpster.

J.T. turned to Daisy, giving her that helpless puppy-dog look that must have been successful in the past. They'd been dating. Well, they'd been sort of dating. Daisy had confessed to me that date number one had been awkward and without any sort of lightning-bolt attraction on her part. J.T. was enough of a detective to notice this and had dialed back his wooing. He was attentive, flattering, and came up with fun, interesting date ideas, but was clearly keeping his hands to himself. It was working. She'd never admit it, but Daisy was relaxing in his company and enjoying how the not-quite-a-romance was proceeding on her own terms.

But the soft spot she was forming for my boss still had its limits.

"I'm not getting in that dumpster, Gator Pierson." She folded her arms across her chest. "Not happening."

J.T. sighed and pulled a wad of bills out of his pocket, turning to one of the two college kids he'd recruited to be his camera crew. He was pretty cheap, and I was sure he was paying them in "career-enhancing credit on the film," so I was surprised when he stripped a ten off the stack of cash and held it out to one of the kids.

"Ten bucks if you put the brown wig on and get into the dumpster."

The kid eyed the ten, then the wad of cash. "Twenty."

J.T. thought about that for a second. "Okay, twenty."

The kid put down the broom-handle boom mic and snatched a brown wig out of a box of props that J.T. had bought at a going-out-of-business costume shop. With an agile leap, he was up and over the edge of the dumpster.

"Ugh. It stinks in here."

Didn't I know it.

"Gator" ignored him. "Okay, Daisy, you creep forward, snatch the tablet out of his hands, then close the lid on him."

"Hey! I didn't agree to be closed in here—"

"You." J.T. turned to the camera guy. "Film it so all you can see is his hands and his wig hair. We'll just slap 'reenactment' on it and maybe do a blurry filter and hope no one notices."

It was a YouTube video. No one would notice. And if they did, they wouldn't care. Gator Pierson had gotten quite a following on his channel. His initial ten viewers had jumped to nearly two thousand over the summer, most of them probably locals. Even so, the modest success had meant J.T. spent almost as much time on his videos as he did on actual investigating. Good thing I had my license now, because someone was going to need to do the work around the office.

Bitter? A little bit. Everyone had a hobby, but why did my boss's have to involve me reliving near-death experiences?

"Annnnnd, action!"

We stood still, because the boom mic that J.T. was now holding had a habit of picking up ambient sounds. Daisy crept forward and snatched the tablet from the fake-Kay's hands, slamming the lid on the poor kid's head.

"Ow."

The expletive was followed up by a few choice curse words. J.T. sighed, clapping a hand across his forehead. "Cut. I guess we can edit that out, or just have the reenactment clip silent with a voiceover commentary." He looked over at us, then handed the boom mic to the cameraman, going over to place the garbage bags on top of the dumpster.

"It's really hot in here. And it smells horrible."

"Almost done," J.T. replied, motioning to the waitress who was leaning against the building, waiting for her scene. It was a good thing J.T. knew the owner; otherwise I'm sure the taco joint would have refused to loan him a staff member for his video. J.T. scurried over to the cameraman and took the boom mic from him.

"Annnnnd, action!"

The waitress sashayed down the stairs like a runway model, posed in an exaggerated hands-on-hips pout as she regarded the dumpster, then began to carefully remove the bags. When the sound guy popped the lid open, she jumped back with a fake scream, hands across her chest.

"Cut." J.T. looked at his watch. "We'll do the rest in the office tomorrow. Daisy, are you still on board to do the perp-walk scene?"

Daisy sniffed. "Are you still buying me wine and steak at Etienne's this weekend?"

My boss gave my best friend the sappiest glance I'd ever seen. "Absolutely. Whether or not you do the perp-walk scene."

That was totally the right thing to say.

Daisy turned to the side to hide a smile. "Yeah, I'll do the perp walk. And yeah, I'm totally going with you to Etienne's this weekend."

Oh my. My friend was falling for J.T.'s charm. I had no idea my boss even had charm, but clearly he was making an effort with Daisy that no one else had seemed to be worthy of.

J.T. grinned at Daisy, then glanced down at his watch again. "You pack up the props and bring them by tomorrow at two." He waved at the two young guys—one holding the camera and the other climbing out of the dumpster—before turning to me.

"Can you run by the courthouse and pick up a packet from the Records Division for me? I need to get back and meet with a client."

A client! I crossed my fingers and hoped it was something interesting, although Locust Point was a small town. Outside of the odd rash of murders we'd had lately, the most common crime was jaywalking or an occasional DWI. With my luck, this would be a missing dog investigation or a someone violating their HOA.

Without waiting for my response, J.T. turned to Daisy, that sappy smile back on his face. "Are you free tonight?"

And just like that, the doors slammed on my friend's expression. "I...I have plans. But I'll see you this weekend. For Etienne's."

"It's the sneak-peek opening of Kitty Harlem's Kat Kafe. Five cats from the shelter will be there for yoga-with-cats."

I blinked in surprise, eyeing my boss and wondering if he seriously did yoga. He didn't look like he did yoga, but I didn't want to indulge in stereotyping. Either way, Daisy looked just as shocked as I did, then bit back a smile.

"Yoga? With...cats?"

J.T. shrugged, shoving his hands in his pockets and attempting a casual posture. "It's a new thing. I think it's supposed to relax you or be more Zen or something. And the cats are all up for adoption. I know the owner, and she's big into cat rescue, population control for feral cat colonies and all that."

Now *I* was interested. I'd never had a cat in my life before Taco, but the little guy had turned me into a huge fan of the species. I wondered if I could tag along on this date.

"Oh." Daisy was melting before my very eyes. "I didn't know you liked yoga. Or cats."

J.T. gave her one of those sheepish little-boy looks that always worked for men no matter their age. "I've never done yoga in my life. Or had a cat."

I felt like I was watching the early part of a Hallmark movie.

"I… I can reschedule that thing I had to do tonight. Are you going to actually do yoga? With the cats?"

"I don't think the cats actually do yoga," J.T. said. "I think they just wander around and purr and stuff. But yes, I'll do the yoga."

I didn't know who tutored J.T. in the art of romance, but he or she deserved a medal. For a guy who'd never been married, he sure knew the way to a woman's heart—and it wasn't just steak and wine at Etienne's. He was willing to risk looking like an utter fool to do something Daisy liked. He'd gone out of his way to find an activity she was sure to love, even though it meant he was going to have to put on sweat pants and try to contort his body on a mat for half an hour. With cats.

Daisy's face bloomed with her smile. "Well then, I will definitely go. What time?"

"I'll pick you up at seven?" He looked at his watch again and shot her an apologetic grimace. "I gotta run."

"Go." She waved him on. "I'll see you at seven."

I watched J.T. jog for his car and watched the two guys hauling their gear and the box of props off to an ancient, rusted Corolla. Then I turned to Daisy.

"So….?"

She blushed. "Okay. He's fun. He's so nice. I feel safe with him, like he's rock solid, like he's the kind of man who would put me first. I like that. It's a novel experience for me."

We slowly made our way to our own vehicles, down the little set of stairs into the parking garage, and past the spot where Luanne Trainor had died. She was still there, a blur of smoke and shadow, slowly making her way to the exit, hovering near the steps, then collapsing into a heap. As we walked past the tableau, I shuddered with the cold, turning to see the shadowy figure vanish to appear about ten feet away from the exit. Poor thing. I wondered if this really was her ghost, or just some weird echo imprint of the violence of her death. That her spirit was still here going through the motions nearly a month after she'd died worried me. Eli's ghost was still in my house, and I assumed Holt's was down haunting Atlanta and the football team. Mr. Peter still occasionally lurked across the street. I'd always assumed that ghosts vanished once I'd sent their murderers to jail, but it seems some of them had other agendas and priorities.

Which meant I couldn't do anything else for Luanne Trainor except avoid this parking garage in the future and hope that eventually she drifted off to the light.

"Yoga with cats, though," Daisy continued, absolutely unaware of the ghostly scene playing out behind us. "That's pretty impressive. I can't believe J.T. came up with that. Yoga. And cats."

"He's growing on you?" I asked with a grin.

She winced. "You make him sound like a tumor, or a big mole. But yes, he's growing on me. I've known him since I was a kid, but we never really ran in the same circles, so I didn't really *know* him. In high school, I was punk, and he was...I don't know. He was just some generic guy. I knew he was there, but he wasn't hot or cool or anything."

"And you never ran into him after high school?" I prodded.

She shrugged. "On occasion. J.T. never hit my radar as a guy I'd ever date. I was kind of shocked when he asked me out."

"I get the impression he's liked you for a while," I told her, unlocking my car.

"I don't know. Maybe. He's never expressed anything before this summer."

I wondered if me working with J.T. had brought Daisy to his notice. Sometimes an old crush could be revived when someone circled back into your life with enough proximity to make a relationship a possibility.

"So how much of a punk were you in high school?" I asked.

Daisy pulled out her phone and scrolled, turning it to me when she got to the picture.

Wow. In the photo, my friend was a statuesque, leggy, platinum blonde with an edgy hairdo and bold makeup and attire. She had a t-shirt slashed to where it was a miracle it had remained on her body. She was toothpick thin, with acne and raccoon-thick eyeliner. Her hair was shaved on the sides and up in a stiff Mohawk. Each ear was pierced five times from what I could see, which wasn't the norm in the late 70s from what I remembered, although I'd been the nerdy yearbook committee girl, not an edgy punk one.

"Those piercings closed up before I graduated." She laughed. "My friend did them with a needle and some ice cubes, and they never healed right. They were always infected, and it was impossible to get a good night's sleep on those things. I can't tell you how much agony it was to have someone try to ram a sewing needle through your ear cartilage, ice numb or not."

I winced. "Can I confess that I wore clip-on earrings until college? Even then, I didn't tell my mom I'd gotten them pierced until years later."

She put the phone back in her pocket. "My dad was never around, and Mom was so tanked on vodka and valium that she didn't know whether I was home or not half the time. But yeah, J.T. and I weren't exactly compatible back then. I'm not sure we're compatible now."

"Do you enjoy being with him?"

Her expression softened. "Yes. I do."

"Then stop worrying about it. Worst case, you've found a friend—although I'll admit I'm a bit jealous about the yoga-with-cats thing. Best case, you develop feelings for him and take it to the next level."

She sighed. "He wants it to go there. I don't know if it ever will on my part. I feel like I'm taking advantage of him. Mooching. I mean, Etienne's isn't cheap. And he's actually going to do *yoga* for Pete's sake. I don't want to lead him on."

I fixed her with a stern look. "Daisy, J.T. is a grown man. He is fully capable of walking away from this. You've made your hesitancy clear. Whether he accepts that and continues to see you is his choice, not yours. Respect that he can make that decision for himself."

It was as if a weight fell from her shoulders. She turned to me with a smile. "You're right. I do enjoy his company, and I've got to say this yoga-with-cats thing really raises the man up a few notches in my affections."

I climbed into my car. "Just relax and stop worrying about Gator Pierson. If he can face down some dude threatening to fill him full of bird shot for repo'ing his F-250, then he can be patient with whatever may or may not be happening between you two."

Daisy gave me the thumbs-up, then practically skipped to her own car as I pulled away. And yes, I *was* still jealous about the yoga and cats.

CHAPTER 2

I swung by the courthouse on my way back to the office, leaving everything in my car except for my ID so I didn't get held up at the metal detectors or have to deal with leaving my phone at the security booth. The Records Division didn't have the copies ready for J.T. yet, so I climbed the stairs to the second floor and wandered around the halls outside the courtrooms, looking at the posted dockets to see who had what cases going on today.

There was a whole lot going on in traffic court, and a dozen or so people milling about the hallway. A few of them were in hushed conversation with suited lawyers, while others stared numbly at the clock, waiting for their moment in court. I poked my head in for a few moments, quietly edging into a rear row. After three speeding cases where the defendants tried to claim they were running late to church as an excuse, I got bored and left. I was pretty sure the judge wished he could leave as well from the weary expression on the man's face.

I made my way past two other courtrooms, only to see that Judge Beck was in the last one, handling criminal cases. I eyed the docket, realizing that the poor guy had a full day's work still ahead of him, and turned to leave. Hmm. Another ten minutes until my copies would be ready, and I really wasn't thrilled about just walking the halls or sitting through more traffic court.

Opening the door, I snuck in, slipping into one of the back booths and giving an apologetic glance to the three women who scooted over for me. The judge didn't even look up, but I was sure he was used to lawyers and others coming and going during the trials and didn't let it distract him. A few seconds in, and it became evident that this defendant was on trial for theft—workplace theft, to be exact. It seemed the woman facing the court with a defeated slump of her shoulders was accused of making off with over sixteen thousand dollars in automotive parts from the local Toyota dealer that had been her employer up until the last month. I'd been envisioning the woman driving off with a couple of engines in the back of her truck, but as the prosecutor laid out the evidence, it became clear that the thief was far more subtle and sneaky then I'd imagined.

She'd been charging customer accounts for the parts, then crediting the accounts but not returning the part to inventory. They were items that I imagined would be easily resalable—brake rotors, belts and hoses, cases of synthetic oil, batteries.

Allegedly, I mean. Because innocent until proven guilty.

I sat riveted, until I realized I needed to get my copies from the Records Division and hustle myself back to the job that was paying my bills, so I snuck out the door and headed down the stairs, resolved to ask Judge Beck about the case later tonight.

On the way, I ran into someone I'd not expected to see—Violet Smith. She did a double take that mirrored mine, then laughed and pulled me into a hug.

"Mrs. Carrera! Are you here on business? It's so good to see you!"

"Just picking up some copies. How are things in Tax Assessments?" I'd given Violet a reference, completely impressed with the mock interview she'd done with me and had been thrilled that she'd gotten the job with the county tax office. It wasn't her dream job, but it was one step on the pathway. This was a full-time job right out of college with a nice salary and good benefits and it would look great on her resume when she had enough experience to begin applying for jobs in financial audits either in the public or private sector.

"Oh, I'm loving it there. Let me know when you're going to be down here again, and we can do lunch." She gave me another hug, then ran up the stairs.

I watched her go, then headed down, wondering how often I would be heading to the courthouse for various tasks. J.T. spent a lot of time here, I assumed doing bail paperwork for clients and schmoozing as well as pulling records for various cases. Now that I was an actual investigator and not just doing skip tracing, maybe I'd be able to do the same. It would be fun to meet Violet for lunch occasionally, and perhaps Judge Beck as well if his schedule allowed.

The young man in the Records Division was just sliding my copies into a manila envelope as I walked in. I took them with a smile, waved at the guys manning the metal detector at the door, and headed for work and the stack of skip traces waiting for me there.

There was a woman sitting in J.T.'s client chair when I walked in. She looked to be in her mid-thirties with the immaculately groomed appearance and vengeful expression of someone going through a divorce. Beside her sat an enormous file box. I blinked in surprise because J.T. had been hurrying back for a consult on a drug possession bond, and this woman didn't look at all like someone whose brother or sister might need bail for that sort of thing.

Although I supposed even immaculately groomed, upper-middle-class middle--aged women had addicts in their family.

"Kay, this is Ms. Marissa Thompson. Mrs. Thompson, Kay Carrera is an investigator with our firm. She specializes in the internet research such as skip trace and credit review."

Mrs. Thompson turned to me with a tight smile. "Here you go." She motioned to the giant file box.

I gave J.T. my best "What's going on?" look.

"Mrs. Thompson's divorce attorney suggested she contact an investigator to dig into her husband's finances. She has a suspicion that he has a significant source of income that he's been hiding from her."

Ah. Hence the enormous box and the fact that J.T. had lobbed this case my way. I read between the lines. If the divorce attorney wasn't taking this on and contracting the investigation themselves, it meant they thought there was nothing to Ms. Thompson's suspicions. Better for her to go hire her own investigator that she could berate as incompetent fools when they turned up nothing then have her blame her attorney.

Us. Berate *us* as incompetent fools. No, actually it was me she'd be berating. I was J.T.'s sacrificial lamb on this one, but I guess that was what happened when you had a shiny new PI license and worked for the illustrious Gator Pierson.

"And a mistress," the woman added. "I'm pretty sure there's a mistress somewhere. But the urgency is to find any hidden assets, because the moment I have Spencer served with the divorce paperwork, we'll never find it."

Actually, a good forensic accountant could still find the money. Closing bank accounts didn't wipe out any history of their existence, and there would always be records of transfers and withdrawals. There were methods of laundering ill-gotten gains and making them appear legitimate but hiding large sums in this day and age wasn't easy unless you resorted to cash-only transactions and hid it all under the mattress. Even then, actually buying anything significant with the cash would become problematic. Showing up at a real estate closing with half a million in a briefcase would get you sent to a bank for a certified check—where the cash would be traceable once more. And you'd probably receive a friendly visit from some federal agency to boot.

But I doubted that was the case here. Gambling winnings? Siphoning earnings into a little side account for the mistress? A quick credit and social media search should point me in the right direction.

"What caused you to be suspicious that your husband had hidden assets, Ms. Thompson?" I asked.

"There have been little things over the last year, a bit more lavish spending than usual. We have a joint checking account, and Spencer handles the finances, so I just assumed he got a raise or a bigger bonus, but when I started looking at the statements, I saw his payroll deposits haven't changed significantly in the last three years. If anything, they're slightly smaller."

"Is there a savings account somewhere he could have been depositing to?"

She nodded. "Yes, but I checked that. It hasn't had more than the usual monthly deposit in five years. There's an auto transfer of three hundred dollars a month into it from our checking account, but no withdrawals."

"Do you have his wage statements from his employer?" I asked, thinking that maybe Spencer *had* gotten a big raise, and had directed his company to deposit the extra amount in a separate, personal account. It was a common tactic for those who saw divorce looming on the horizon and shuddered at the idea of dividing their assets right down the middle.

"No, he doesn't get paper paycheck stubs or statements and I don't have access to log in to his payroll site at work. There's no way I could get that information without tipping him off that I'm about to file for divorce."

I grimaced, realizing she was right. Her divorce attorney could request them as part of the case, but by then the money could have vanished, allegedly spent on consumables.

"Is there anything else that made you suspect he'd been hiding money from you?" I pressed. "Gambling? A side job? An elderly relative of his that died and you suspect might have willed him money?"

"I've never seen him gamble, and with the long hours he works, I'd never know if there was a side job or a mistress, but either of those is possible. The inheritance thing is unlikely. Spencer's family isn't particularly well off, and no one has died in the last five years that I know of." Again, she motioned to that intimidatingly large box. "Oh, there is one other thing. Back in August, we went out to Stella's for a dinner with two other couples. Spence had overindulged a bit on the scotch and paid the entire check." She grimaced with the painful memory. "I about had a heart attack, because six people at Stella's...you can imagine what that check was."

Yes, I could. Eli and I had been there once twelve years ago for an anniversary dinner. I'd joked that we would need to take out a second mortgage just to pay for our meal.

"But it's not there." She paused for effect, waving a hand at the box. "Spence put it on a card, and I remember thinking it didn't look like our usual one, but at the time, I didn't worry about it. But the charge didn't show up on either our bank statement or our credit card statement. Two thousand dollars, Ms. Carrera. That transaction would stand out, and I can't find it."

"A company credit card?" I suggested. She gave me a look that made it clear she was doubting my competence.

"He would have been fired. Spencer works for Fullbright and Mason. Investment firms aren't exactly loose in their accounting practices, and his expense account is tightly audited—as are all the consultants'. I think he may be moon-lighting, that he's got some lucrative business on the side and has been hiding it from both me and his employer."

Which would violate both his non-compete and the trust of his soon-to-be-ex-wife. I eyed the box and straightened my shoulders, foreseeing a lot of long nights ahead of me.

"Is there anything else that made you suspect he had hidden assets?" I asked.

"No, just a wife's intuition. But it's not just the finances I want you to look into." She squirmed. "I think...I mean, I know divorce is no-fault in this state, and it wouldn't matter if he was having an affair, but I'm pretty sure he is. But I can't find any proof of it."

I was completely confused. "So, you think he's having an affair, but there's no proof? No receipts for flowers or hotel charges on your credit card, or shirts smelling like someone else's perfume?"

"No." Mrs. Thompson looked downright embarrassed. "But he was talking to someone named Tracy last year, and when I came in he looked uncomfortable and ended the phone call with some awkward excuses about calling her later. I looked up the number on our cell phone bill and did a search. He'd been calling her a few times a week. Then, six months ago, I walked in on him having a heated argument over the phone with someone. When I checked the phone record, it was the same number."

Wow. Paranoid much? I was a bit aghast at how suspi-cious she'd been and how much investigative work she'd already done over the course of a year or more. Wasn't a marriage supposed to be based on trust? Although with Eli, I'd always had a reason to trust. Who knew what sort of person Spencer Thompson was that his wife was diligently checking phone records and bank accounts, building a case for her divorce for at least a year in advance?

"Did you ever call that number?" I asked, because someone that meticulous surely would have phoned the alleged mistress and confronted her.

"Yes, but it went to voice mail, and it was one of those generic 'please leave a message' robotic voices. No one ever called me back, and I was worried that if I kept calling her, she'd tell Spencer and he'd run off to Jamaica with her and our entire bank account or something."

"Was your relationship always this…uneasy?" I didn't want to insult the woman, but clearly there was something fundamentally wrong in their marriage.

A muscle twitched in her jaw and for a moment I thought she wasn't going to answer me. "Spencer was always a businessman first. When I met him, we were in our early twenties, and I knew then that he was going places. The man was sharp. He could spot an opportunity from a mile away and be ready to take advantage of it. I loved that about him. Being with him was exciting and exhilarating. I loved his brilliance. Then about five years ago, I realized that we weren't partners, that any opportunity he spotted, he'd take advantage of regardless of whether it benefitted me or not. I realized that he'd happily leave me in the dust if he could score big money on his own."

"So, for five years you were okay living with that?"

Her face hardened and she took a deep breath before responding. "Yes. I kept a wary eye on things but staying with Spencer was still a better deal than going forward alone, and I still loved him. But this Tracy thing…I can't tolerate him cheating on me. I mean, cheating on me financially is bad enough, but for him to have another woman on the side? I read the writing on the wall and figured I better divorce him before he managed to drain our accounts and run off with this floozy."

I nodded. "Thank you for your honesty. It makes my job a lot easier."

She nudged the box toward me. "Please let me know if you have any questions. My lawyer is already poised to begin the divorce process, but I'm holding off, worried about Spence having significant assets elsewhere, so time is of the essence here."

I gave her a sympathetic smile. "I completely understand. I'll go through this tonight as well as search my usual online resources. Questions or not, I'll contact you tomorrow morning to update you on my progress." After running it all by J.T., of course. I might be the one who knew skip-tracing and internet research, but he was the experienced investigator while I was still very much wet behind my ears.

Marissa Thompson pulled a card from her purse and handed it to me with a flourish of manicured nails. Then she stood and shook my hand. J.T. escorted her to the door, bowing and scraping like the woman was the Queen of England.

I waved the little card at him once Mrs. Thompson had left. "So, she's either Locust Point Royalty, or paying us an insane hourly rate for this."

He grinned. "The latter. Now get to work."

I hauled the box over to my desk and started to go through the contents, happy to see that whoever made the copies had sorted them and clipped them into neat stacks. Bank statements. Credit card statements. A whole bunch of receipts. Some handwritten notes. A sheet of paper with logins and passwords. Cell phone numbers. I gave it all a quick look, then sat down at my computer, figuring I'd do what I did best and check this guy out online before diving into the paperwork. Mrs. Thompson had included a sheet in the box with personal information on her husband—date of birth, college attended and date of graduation, a resume, addresses for the last three houses they'd lived in, names and ages of living family members, and Social Security number.

The first thing that struck me was that Spencer Thompson's social media was completely sanitized and professional. I wasn't surprised given that he made a living as a financial consultant, and a certain amount of salesmanship was expected in that job. He was all over every social media site, his posts filled with handy financial tips, news on stocks to watch, and pictures of him schmoozing at nearly every business-themed social event in the county. The latest one was a Chamber of Commerce happy hour where he was flanked by a real estate professional and a mortgage lender. Another picture from the same event had him next to a name I recognized—County Clerk Patrice Defoe. Her picture with a little brass nameplate was up on the wall at the courthouse right next to the Records Division. I made a mental note to ask Judge Beck if he knew Spencer Thompson. I wouldn't have thought they ran in the same social circles, but the guy did seem to get around, rubbing elbows with everyone of interest in the county. How odd that I'd never heard his name mentioned before today, but then again, what use would I have for a financial services consultant? Up until Judge Beck moved in, I was more likely to be needing a bankruptcy attorney.

I looked at the pictures, paging back through several years to see if there were any particular individuals he seemed to be more in the company of—especially any women named Tracy in the tags. There was no Tracy, although Spencer did seem to hang with a lot of mortgage lenders and real estate people, one guy from Piedmont mortgage in particular. I chalked that up more to the events he was attending and the type of professional crowd they would draw. Lenders, realtors, and financial consultants all needed to grow their client base, and I knew that partnerships between them often ended in much-needed business referrals.

From the social media search, I moved on to his company website, pulling up the page for the consultants. Spencer Thompson, it seemed, specialized in estate planning and financial matters specific to those in or approaching retirement. Like everything else I'd seen so far, the photos and the bio were strictly business-like. There was nothing on a judicial case search beyond a few old speeding tickets. His credit report was pristine with no sign of anything that would indicate he was secretly applying for credit cards behind his wife's back. With a sigh, I glanced at the clock and decided to dig into the more intimidating paperwork in the box.

Armed with a highlighter and a notepad, I got to work. I quickly realized this this was a joint checking account, and that the Thompsons appeared to use their debit card for everything they bought. There were multiple convenience store purchases for a couple of dollars, and someone seemed to have a bit of a Starbucks habit. Overwhelmed with the volume, and unable to see any pattern through all the noise, I decided to concentrate on the deposits, plowing through the early statements and highlighting them by source. Spencer started at Fullbright and Mason five years ago, but Marissa had only included the last three years of deposits. Finally, I sat back and stretched. Five o'clock. J.T. was starting to pack up, but I was thinking I might stay an extra hour and finish going through at least the deposits. Might as well since this was all on Marissa Thompson's dime.

"Found anything yet?" J.T. asked as he stuffed a few files in an ancient hard-sided briefcase.

"The only thing so far is that Spencer's direct deposit amount changed two years ago," I told him. "It's not a huge amount—only a few hundred each check. It only adds up to roughly eight or nine thousand. I mean, I'd definitely want half of that in a divorce, but I figured it would be more from the way his wife was talking."

J.T. pursed his lips. "Could there be another explanation for the deposit variation? He upped his 401k contribution? A raise in the company health insurance premiums or something?"

"The start of it doesn't coincide with open enrollment, so I'm thinking no on the benefits explanation. It could be some kind of change in retirement contributions. That could happen mid-year."

"Still, he could have used that eight or nine thousand to start an online gambling empire, or lucrative day trading, or something else," J.T. suggested. "If the guy is one hell of a poker player, then eight thousand could have quickly become a few hundred thousand."

"If so, there has to be some trace of it somewhere. PayPal or some online account, maybe?"

"Possibly. If you knew where that few hundred was being deposited, it would be a start."

I sighed in frustration. "But for that, I'd need to see his paycheck stubs or get into his online payroll system from work."

"We'll eventually have paycheck stubs," J.T. told me. "He'll need to provide them for the divorce discovery process."

True, but Mrs. Thompson wanted to find these hidden assets before she served her husband with the papers. I'd need to do without.

"Lock up when you leave?" J.T. shot me a grin. "And keep track of your hours. The word of the day is 'billable.'"

"Got it. And have fun doing yoga with cats." I laughed at the look on his face.

"So...how badly am I going to humiliate myself trying to bend into positions I haven't done since my twenties? Or ever?"

"Badly. Make sure you bring your sense of humor." I saw his frown deepen and took pity on him. "Daisy doesn't want someone—friend or otherwise—who's perfect and skilled at everything. She appreciates people who are willing to get outside their comfort zones and try new things even if it makes them look foolish. And she really appreciates people who take an interest in the things she does. You don't have to make yoga a daily thing, but the fact that you're giving it a shot makes all the difference."

"And cats?"

I nearly bounced in my chair. "I *know*! I'm so jealous. I enjoy yoga, but yoga with *cats*? I wonder if they come up and rub against you and purr as you're doing the poses, or if they just wander around. I'd probably fall over, I'd be so busy checking out the kitties."

Who would have thought I'd become such a fan of cats? Before I'd adopted Taco, I'd been ambivalent toward them, but now I couldn't see my life without a furry feline in it. But one look at my boss made me realize not everyone shared my enthusiasm.

"You don't like cats?"

He grimaced. "I had a beagle growing up. Does that count?"

"No, it doesn't. How do you not like cats?" I'll admit that last question sounded a bit belligerent, but I thought of Taco and couldn't believe that J.T. wouldn't love my little guy.

"It's not that I don't like them. They don't seem to like me. I go to pet them, and they bite me and run away. Or they reach up and claw my leg. They jump up on the counters and knock things over, and…well, they don't listen. They don't sit or come when they're called. And when you tell them to go away, they just stare at you."

"You just haven't met the right cat," I told him. "I'm sure there will be one or two at yoga tonight that will capture your heart. You said they're all adoptable. Maybe you'll end up taking one home."

"That's what I'm afraid of," he muttered. "Daisy's going to talk me into adopting one of those things, I just know it."

I bit back a smile. "Well, then you need to stay strong. I've heard you say 'no' before, J.T. It's a word in your vocabulary."

"Not where Daisy is concerned," he admitted.

"Just tell Daisy you're not ready for that sort of commitment yet, or that you want to wait and make sure you're choosing the perfect cat." I waved him toward the door. "Be creative. Think on your feet. And get going. You'll need to change before you go, because there's no way you're going to manage a downward dog in those khakis."

I watched him leave, shouldering his briefcase as if he were about to head into battle, then I turned my attention back to the stacks of bank statements on my desk.

$\mathcal{I}$ dragged myself home well after six and found an empty house. That wasn't terribly surprising on weeks when the judge didn't have his kids and stayed at the courthouse late, but this was his week with Henry and Madison. When the kids were here, Judge Beck rearranged his schedule to pick them up after school, which meant he was usually home before five. Though, with the kids' after school activities, an occasional mid-week game or a practice running late would throw off the schedule.

At least Taco was home to greet me at the door, although the cat was clearly more interested in me putting food in his bowl than delivering any loving greeting. I'd taken to letting him outside when I got home, knowing he'd be back promptly in time for dinner, but running late had put me right at the hour I usually fed him and no amount of urging was going to get him out the door.

"Come on, boy. I'll get your dinner." I made my way to the dining room, somehow managing to not trip over the cat weaving around my feet. Depositing my laptop case and an armful of files, I bent down to pick up Taco. Better to carry him into the kitchen then risk breaking a hip because my cat tried to kill me over a late dinner.

After Taco was happily scarfing down his food, I made a sandwich for myself and surveyed the contents of my cupboard, deciding that after working late, an evening of baking and knitting was in order.

Scones? No, I'd made a double batch yesterday, and there was still a dozen or so left. Yeast-raised cinnamon and raisin bread? I eyed the clock and decided that with the rising time for the dough, I'd be up past midnight if I made that recipe.

Pumpkin bars. It was still September, but not too early for this fall favorite. I pulled out the eggs, sugar, oil, flour, and spices, then found the jar of home-canned pumpkin that Bonita Sedgewick had given me after Eli had died. The giant basket had included frozen casseroles, potpourri, canned pumpkin from her garden, and baked goods. The casseroles and baked goods had been consumed long ago, but I'd been waiting for fall to find something to do with the canned pumpkin.

It had been put up in chunks, so I drained it and ran it through my blender on puree before adding it to the rest of my ingredients. While the bars baked, I gathered the cream cheese, butter, powdered sugar, and vanilla to make the frosting. Thirty minutes later, the bars were cooling from the oven, safely barricaded from an inquisitive Taco, while I turned to eye my knitting.

At the rate I was going on these Christmas shawl projects, they'd end up being Easter gifts. I grabbed the basket, pulled a catnip treat from the drawer to bribe Taco to stay away from the baked goods, and headed into the parlor. A shadow formed in the corner of the room, moving closer as I sat and pulled my knitting from the basket. It had gotten to the point where I sometimes didn't consciously think of the ghost I'd come to believe was my late husband, Eli. He was just here, a comforting presence. Occasionally, I'd talk to him and tell him about my day, but most times I just enjoyed having him nearby. Even when his shadowy form didn't appear in the corner of my vision, I still felt him about the house.

Would he always be here? There was a time when I clung to that thought like a lifeline, but now, increasingly, the idea that his spirit would never be at rest bothered me.

"I'll be okay," I whispered to him as I organized my yarn and eyed the pattern. "I miss you. I love you. But I'm not alone like I'd feared I'd be. I'll be okay."

The shadow shifted closer, its presence sending goosebumps up my arms. Taco paused in his attack of the catnip toy to eye the ghost, then moved his herb-laced mouse to the other side of the room. I closed my eyes and imagined a time before the accident, when Eli and I would sit on this couch and read, or listen to records, when we took vacation and went out to dinner at fancy places like Stella's, when it seemed our happily ever after would go on...well, forever.

But those were memories. We never know what the future may bring. And right now, I had a Christmas gift to knit.

Three rows of lacy blue shawl later, the shadow had vanished. I sat the knitting down and headed in to ice the pumpkin bars. I'd just put them in the refrigerator when the front door opened and I heard an excited chorus of voices. I also smelled the wonderful aroma of pizza.

"Ms. Kay! Ms. Kay!" Madison danced into the kitchen, doing a pirouette as she passed the center island. "Dad let me drive home!"

The girl waved a little card at me. I took it and admired her learner's permit before handing it back.

"We almost died," Henry teased as he sat a giant box of pizza on the counter. "Dad's outside, checking the SUV for scratches and dents."

"I didn't hit anything," Madison protested. "And anyone would have run over the curb. It's a tight turn."

"Well, you just about gave old Mrs. Steadman a heart attack," Henry told her with a grin. "She thought you were coming straight for her. Two more inches and she would have had to jump into the bushes to keep from getting run over."

"She did just fine, Henry," Judge Beck scolded as he came into the kitchen. "She just clipped that corner. I've done it, and so has your mother. And Mrs. Steadman was at least twenty feet away from us."

I bit back a smile, because in spite of the judge's words, he did seem unusually pale right now.

"You'll change your tune the first time you want me to drive you somewhere," Madison countered, waving her learner's permit at her brother. "Six months and I'll be a licensed driver."

"You still won't be able to drive anyone under the age of eighteen unless there's another licensed driving adult in the car," Henry shot back. "Not for another six months."

"That's still three years before you'll be getting behind the wheel. I can hear it now: 'Oh Mads, can you drop me off at the arcade? Can you pick me up from Jason's house?'"

"Not unless I had a death wish," Henry shot back.

"Enough." Judge Beck fixed each of the children in turn with a stern glare. "It's almost eight o'clock. Homework in your rooms, and lights out by ten. Got it?"

There was a chorus of "got its," then a scramble to grab drinks from the fridge before the two shouldered their backpacks and climbed the stairs, both continuing to argue about Madison's driving ability.

"Spill it," I said to the judge as I poured myself a glass of iced tea. "Is she really that bad?"

"She's probably a better driver than I was at her age," he

admitted. "She's very careful, just inexperienced. I, on the other hand, was too busy trying to look cool and check out the other cars and pedestrians for attractive women to pay attention to where I was going."

I laughed. "How many cars did you total before the age of twenty?"

"Clearly, I had a guardian angel looking over me because there were no serious accidents, but I did my fair share of driving over curbs and even took out a few shrubs. There was that time I took off the passenger side mirror trying to get Kelly O'Connell to notice me, though. My buddy and I tried to reattach it to no avail. I lied to my parents that there had been a hit-and-run while it was parked at the grocery store, but they found out the truth and I wound up grounded for two months as well as having to work off the cost of the repair."

"But did Kelly O'Connell notice you?"

"Noticed me. Laughed at me. Promptly went out with some football jock instead of me." Judge Beck smiled ruefully. "I wasn't always this suave ladies' man you see before you now."

I chuckled and headed into the dining room with my tea, the judge following behind me. He'd said that somewhat self-mockingly, as if he'd never considered himself to be a suave ladies' man, but I found it hard to believe someone as good looking as Judge Beck was often turned down for a date.

The pair of us settled in, me with my tea and my huge box of files and the judge with his leather briefcase and stacks of paperwork. I smiled at what was becoming our nightly routine of working across from each other at my dining room table.

"J.T. had me swing by the Records Division today. They didn't have my files ready, so I wandered around and peeked in on your courtroom," I told him.

He sorted through his stack of papers. "Which case? The sentencing modification, or the theft trial?"

"The theft. It was fascinating to see you doing your King Solomon thing," I teased.

He shot me a sardonic glance. "I'm a Circuit Court Judge. The jury decides guilt or innocence. There's no King Solomon thing, unless you're referring to my keeping the two attorneys from slicing each other in half."

"Okay, referee thing then."

He shook his head. "I'm more like a babysitter than a referee. Mainly I just make sure everyone plays nice in the sandbox. If you wanted to see some King Solomon action, you should have checked out Judge Sanchez on the District Court side. He drew the short straw and had traffic court today."

"I went there first. I didn't count, but it looked like the poor guy had over a hundred cases on his docket today. After the fourth 'I was speeding because I was late for church' excuse, I left."

"I'm pretty sure Judge Sanchez had been wishing he could leave as well. That theft case today should have been his, or at least one of the District Court judges, but it was over five thousand dollars and under thirty, so it fell in that middle gray area. I accused Jorge of lobbing it over to me and was going to give it back, but the defendant wanted a jury trial." He glanced up at me over his glasses. "So that was my day. Listening to a very eloquent attorney first thing in the morning tell me why his client shouldn't serve twenty, then this theft trial that took the entire rest of the day. We were pushing it close. I wasn't sure I'd get done in time to pick the kids up from practice."

"You know you can always call on me if you need back-up." I said it without thinking, then felt myself flush warmer than any hot flash. "In an emergency, I mean. I might be able to help, although probably not today. I worked late and didn't get home until six."

I wasn't their mother. I was the landlord. It wasn't my place for one, and for two, I was afraid of becoming some sort of default unpaid nanny for Judge Beck's children. Yes, I loved them. Yes, I'd do anything for them. But if the judge wanted shared physical custody, he needed to have a fallback plan. It would be too easy for me to land into that role, and I couldn't. I needed to figure out an independent life for myself now that Eli was gone, and that didn't include being Judge Beck's substitute wife.

He shot me a look from over the top of his reading glasses. "I'd only call you if it were an emergency, Kay. If I want joint custody, I need to make this work on my own. Plus, I'm really enjoying these moments together with them. It's amazing what kids open up and say when you're driving them home from school."

"Or teaching them to drive?" I teased.

He grimaced. "Honestly? That shaved five years off my life. We came awfully close to a lamp post in the parking lot, and she went up on another curb turning into the driveway."

Oh my. It seems Madison hadn't learned as much at last week's driver's education class as her father had hoped. I envisioned him white-knuckled in the passenger seat and chuckled.

"I'm sure there will be a few unexplained scrapes and dents in the next few years," I told him.

"Scrapes and dents I can live with. Late-night calls from the side of the road while waiting for a tow truck and/or an ambulance are what I'm afraid of." He peered over my shoulder. "What are you working on tonight? Those look like bank statements."

"They are." I waved my highlighter at him. "I have my first real case as an investigator, and it's...a divorce!"

"Ah. A topic I'm very familiar with. Let me guess, you're deep in the weeds trying to find proof of an affair?"

"Hidden assets," I told him. "And possibly an affair. But mostly hidden assets." I looked up at him. "Um, not to imply anything here, but if you were going to hide some money from your wife, how would you do it?"

He shrugged, pushing aside his paperwork. "Beats me. Heather managed all of our finances and paid the bills. I pulled a couple hundred in cash out every week or two to cover coffee, lunch, the occasional gallon of milk on the way home. That sort of thing."

I blinked, surprised that he managed to spend a few hundred every week or two on coffee and lunches. I spent a little more than that on my total grocery bill. "But if you wanted to, how would you have done it?"

He considered that for a moment, then slowly shook his head. "Diverting any significant part of my paycheck deposit would be too easy to trace. A spouse is going to notice anything more than a hundred or so a month difference in the deposits and ask for the paycheck stubs to be presented during the divorce process. If the money was for an investment I was sure would pay off, I might take out a loan in my own name, then use the profits to set up a separate account after I'd paid the loan back."

"The loan will still show up on your credit report," I reminded him. "If she's suspicious, she'll catch that and wonder what it was for as well as how it got repaid."

"Borrow from friends or family for the investment?"

I nodded and made a note on my pad of paper. "I'll check into that. J.T. thinks it could be gambling wins or he's moonlighting, but I'm not convinced there was an investment or a side business. Right now, all I know is the wife thinks there's hidden assets and that there was an unfamiliar bank or credit card in his name that didn't show on the credit report I pulled."

"Maybe the credit report is wrong?"

My eyebrows shot up. "All three of them? Maybe with an apartment rental or some used car lot loan, but not a credit card. That stuff always gets reported. Always. Unless he's used a stolen identity, and in that case, we'd be dealing with more than divorce here."

The judge looked intrigued. "Do you think he could be involved in something like that? Embezzlement from his work? Stolen credit cards?"

I shook my head but made a quick note on the pad. *Check embezzlement and ID theft.* "I doubt it. He's been at a major investment firm for five years. I'm sure they take their accounting audits pretty seriously. Plus, it would have to be a huge payoff for him to risk a lucrative and promising career like that. The guy looks squeaky clean as far as his online presence, criminal searches, and credit accounts. It's like he's the Ken doll of investment advisors."

Judge Beck narrowed his eyes. "Expense reimbursements."

I blinked in surprise. "Forging them? At a blue-chip investment firm?"

"No, diverting the reimbursements into a separate account." Judge Beck steepled his hands under his chin. "I know ours get processed separately, and they usually come on the non-payroll week. If he's got a few thousand a month in expenses, that could be a lot."

I scribbled it down on the pad. "But that shows up on the W-2, doesn't it? It's been ten years since Eli got a check or a W-2, but I seem to remember there being a box for it."

He nodded. "True, but if they lob all their paperwork over to a tax accountant like everyone else does, the wife may not ever have noticed."

Check W-2s. That should be easy. Marissa should have access to that. And I was trying to ignore the fact that I hadn't needed a tax accountant in over a decade. When Eli was in practice, yes, but after the accident I couldn't justify the expense—especially since there was far more money going out than coming in.

I went back to the tedium of the bank statements, and Judge Beck began looking through his own work. For the next few hours, the only sounds were of flipping papers, scribbling pencils, and the occasional sigh. Finally, at midnight, when my eyesight was beginning to cloud and all the mundane debit charges were starting to blur together, I said a quiet "goodnight" to the judge, scooped up a sleepy Taco, and headed to bed to dream of expense fraud and expensive dinners at Stella's.

CHAPTER 4

_I_ eyed Daisy from between the legs of my downward dog. It was six in the morning. I'd squeaked in just over five hours of sleep last night. With enough coffee, I'd get through the day, but I really couldn't make a habit of these late nights working combined with yoga at dawn—not unless I wanted to be facedown in a nap on my desk by noon.

Daisy, on the other hand, looked energetic and well-rested. Yoga with cats clearly did a body good.

"So? How did it go last night?" I asked as we continued to hold in downward dog.

Daisy giggled. Giggled. It was a sound so out of place coming from my friend that I almost fell over. "I can't believe I got J.T. Pierson to do yoga, let alone yoga in a room full of cats. He even drank a hibiscus ginger kombucha tea afterward."

Sheesh. J.T. wasn't kidding when he said he'd do anything for Daisy. "So, did you talk him into adopting a cat?"

She snorted. "No. Can you imagine J.T. with a cat? He'd be hopeless with the poor thing. Those kitties need a good home, not someone who would probably forget to feed them."

"He wouldn't forget to feed them. He'd just get one of those giant auto-feeders and maybe pay someone to empty the litter once a week." We shifted into a tree pose, and I sighed, glad to be out of the hamstring agony of downward dog.

"Actually, he'd probably be good with a pet," Daisy admitted. "But it would have to be one he really wanted, not one he adopted because he thought it would get him laid."

I laughed. "You do realize it's only you he's pursuing like this? He's not a...what did Madison call it? A player? He's not a player."

Daisy grinned. "No, but you have to admit that if I told him I'd sleep with him, he'd adopt one of those cats in a hot second."

"He'd have a house full of cats if you slept with him," I told her. "You've got the man wrapped around your finger, Daisy. I mean, he actually spent an evening doing yoga. With cats."

She pivoted into a chair pose. "I know. And...well, he is kind of growing on me."

I mirrored her position. "Growing on you? Like a fungus?"

She laughed. "I like him. I enjoy being with him. The attention is so flattering, and he's not pushy or anything. He's just fun, and gentlemanly, and...I don't know. Chivalrous."

I'd never have imagined anyone describing Gator Pierson as chivalrous, but then again, the guy did save me from being shot. Chivalrous worked for me.

"You don't have to rush anything, Daisy," I told her. "Enjoy his company and just see where it goes. You know he has feelings for you, but J.T. is a patient man. And if the

35

answer ends up being 'no,' he'll still have enjoyed the time he's spent with you."

"I kissed him," she confessed in a whisper as she dropped down into a vajra pose.

I nearly passed out from shock as I knelt down. Kissed him? A thrill ran through me, as if I were a teenager again, discussing my friend's stolen chaste smooch behind the bleachers with a boy with a mouth full of braces.

"You *kissed* him?" It came out with a bit of a squeal. I couldn't help it.

Daisy actually blushed. "It was just a quick thing when we were walking down the street to his car after yoga. I just leaned over and kissed him."

"And?" If she left me with this cliffhanger, I'd never forgive her. Well, I'd forgive her, but I might not let her have an extra piece of the pumpkin bars.

She abandoned the yoga to sit cross-legged and yank a few blades of grass from my lawn. "I think it surprised him as much as it did me. He didn't really have time to respond. It was just a quick smooch, then we kept walking to the car."

"He didn't grab you and kiss you senseless? Knock your socks off? Ravish you right there on Third Street?" I demanded, realizing that I'd probably been reading too many of those Luanne Trainor novels.

"He held my hand." Daisy smirked at me, rolling the torn grass between her fingers. "I'm glad he didn't jump me in some crazed act of passion. It would have ruined what was a beautiful, spontaneous moment."

Score one for my boss. It seemed with Daisy, slow and steady did win the race. And letting her set the speed of things was clearly a good thing. I thought for a moment about how I'd want a relationship to proceed at my age. Back in college, Eli and I had been all over each other pretty much like those romance books I'd been reading, but I didn't think

I'd want that at this point in my life. Passion, yes. Definitely. But I wanted passion built on a foundation of friendship and trust. I wanted it to come to a slow boil, to simmer on the stove a bit. The hormones were definitely still there, but like a car that had sat in the garage for too long, it would take the old engine a while to turn over and catch.

"I'm happy for you, Daisy. J.T. is a nice guy, and I'm happy things are working out between you two," I told her, all the while very much aware that I was also envious. I'd buried my beloved husband six months ago. I wasn't ready to fall in love again. But I longed for that closeness, that rush I got when Eli was near me. Even after his accident, when everything had changed between us, I still loved him. I still enjoyed our life together. And I ached to think I might never have that again—with him or anyone else.

"Well, I think after our dinner at Stella's I might just kiss him again." Daisy jumped to her feet, giving me the whole teenager-vibe again and dispelling my sad mood. "Now, come on. You promised me some pumpkin bars, and I'm a big fan of dessert for breakfast."

She wasn't the only one. As we headed through the kitchen door, I caught Judge Beck, coffee cup in one hand, the other holding a pumpkin bar halfway to his mouth.

He lowered the slice with a sheepish grin. "I hope this wasn't for some charity auction. It looked wonderful. I couldn't help myself."

"Go ahead." I waved at him. "It's Cake for Breakfast Day, didn't you know?"

He took a bite then looked down at the pan. "How about we not tell the kids and just eat it all ourselves?"

I pulled two cups from the cabinet. "Glutton. Go wake your children. I'll cut them each a piece."

He headed upstairs and Daisy eyed him appreciatively— eyed his backside appreciatively, that is. I'll admit that Judge

Beck wandering around in pajama bottoms and an old t-shirt was just as much of a wake-me-up as the coffee.

"So, how's the divorce case thing going?" my friend asked, tilting her head and leaning over to catch a final glimpse at Judge Beck climbing the stairs.

"I worked straight through until midnight and couldn't find much of anything." I sighed in frustration as I handed her a pumpkin bar and a mug of coffee. "I'm in over my head, Daisy. I do skip-traces. Credit reports. Social media and internet searches. Case searches across state lines. This is all bank and credit card statements, and I've got no idea what I'm even looking for. I'd just assumed there'd be some huge money transfer in bold red type with a memo that said 'hiding this from my wife.'"

"Ask J.T. for help." She took a swig of the coffee. "You just got your license. He's supposed to be mentoring you or supervising you or something, isn't he?"

I shrugged. "I'll ask, but this isn't really his thing, either. The divorce cases he does usually involve him sitting outside a no-tell motel with a camera. He's an old-school detective, which is why he hired me to do the skip-trace work. This is more in line with my abilities, but I'm just not an accountant. I need someone who really knows what they're looking at and can spot the needle in the haystack of bank statements."

Daisy took a bite of cake and made a series of appreciative noises. "How about Olive?" she mumbled with her mouth full. "She's an accountant."

"Yes, but she's busy with her company's fiscal year end. She couldn't even make it to last Friday's happy hour. Besides, I need someone who does financial audits. That sort of thing."

Wait. I did know someone who had a CPA license and had specialized in audits—specifically in forensic accounting.

And she was young, without the sort of lofty resume that would make J.T. clutch his wallet in alarm.

"I've got an idea," I told Daisy. "I just have to sell it to J.T."

"Yeah, good luck with that." She took another bite of her pumpkin bar, then glanced up at me with a mischievous twinkle in her eyes. "Unless you'd like me to intervene and ask him myself?"

Oh my. I'd created a monster. "No. You save your influence for the important things, like getting homeless cats adopted or a sponsor for the youth center. I'll handle this one."

* * *

I WALKED through the door to the office, plopped the box of paperwork on my desk and faced J.T., hands on my hips. He paused mid-pour of his coffee and shot me a wary glance. "I take it you haven't found a million dollars hidden in a Swiss bank account?"

"I haven't found fifty cents in between the sofa cushions. Three years of bank statements filled with thousands of transactions for every gallon of gas and box of cereal those people ever bought isn't the easiest thing to sort through. I'm in over my head. I want to ask an accountant to look over this," I told J.T. "Specifically, I want to pay Violet Smith fifty bucks to stop by my house tonight and look over this."

My boss scowled. I could see the miserly gears turning in his brain. "Isn't she a kid? Some recent college grad? I appreciate that you're trying to save us a few bucks here, but Mrs. Thompson can't call on a college kid as an expert witness."

No, she couldn't. Violet was twenty-two, just passed her CPA exam, and not two months into a job at the county tax assessors' office. But she had one thing going for her—she was cheap. And I really liked the idea of tossing some money at a girl who was working hard to dig herself out of generations of crushing poverty.

"We'd need to call Mrs. Thompson and get approval for the funds to hire an actual forensic accountant. Is that something you want to do?" I asked.

I knew darned well what his answer to that would be. J.T. was cheap, but there was more to this than pinching a penny or two. Bringing in a forensic accountant would send a very loud message to our client that we couldn't handle this case. Next step would be her wondering why she was paying us at all when she could just go straight to a forensic accountant herself.

"I don't want to waste fifty bucks on some college kid who doesn't know what she's doing," J.T. protested. "You're good at this sort of thing, Kay. I know you can do this yourself."

"I can, but not as quickly as Mrs. Thompson wants it," I countered. "I'm meeting her for coffee in less than an hour to give her a progress report, and I want to at least be able to reassure her that we're going over these statements with a knowledgeable and fine-toothed comb. Fifty bucks. One night. If Violet doesn't find anything, then she's still probably saved you fifty bucks of my time. If she does find something, we'll be able to show our client that we're making progress and doing it fast."

His eyes narrowed as he considered my argument.

"I've got a hunch," I told him. "I think there's something in these bank statements, something small that I'm missing because I'm just not used to wading through all this accounting stuff. I'm not finding anything through my usual avenues. I seriously think the clue is in the bank statements. If I'm wrong, I'm sure you'd rather spend fifty dollars on my mistake than bill Mrs. Thompson for five days' work and tell her we've got nothing. Or spend five hundred dollars, which is what a forensic accounting 'expert' will cost us. If Violet finds something, then we can always check with Mrs. Thompson about paying for a legit audit to back us up."

J.T. sighed, but when he turned to pour his coffee, I knew I'd won. "Fine. Fifty dollars. But I want something tangible by tomorrow morning. Deal?"

I grinned. "Deal."

"And you're meeting with Mrs. Thompson this morning to give her an update? What are you telling her?"

I dropped my purse on my desk and sat down. "That there are no photos so far that show her husband anywhere except at business events, and those were clearly professional. He seems to socialize with a lot of mortgage bankers and real estate agents. Nothing criminal. Nothing shows up in his credit report beyond the joint accounts with his wife, so any credit he's taken out is either too recent to show up, or is under someone else's name, or a company's EIN. I've found some variances in his direct deposit that go back a few years, but without the paycheck stubs, I can't tell if they're a change in benefits, tax withholding, or a redirect of funds, but I noted it down. Next step is to check tax records and do a deeper dive into the bank statements for anything that might indicate a side investment, business, or gambling enterprise. Or a mistress."

J.T. nodded. "Okay. Don't let her pressure you into conjecturing on anything at this point. Stay strictly to the facts and no interpreting them. Divorces are an emotional business, and if you hint at what you think might be going on, she'll take it and run."

"And we'll look like fools. Or I'll look like a fool."

"If she tries to rush you, just let her know that these things normally take months to go through, and we're trying to accomplish it in a week. Then tell her you'll update her daily on our progress."

"Got it." I smirked and watched my boss sip his coffee for a moment. "So…you're going to film the last few scenes of your Luanne Trainor video this morning, right?"

He shot me a narrow-eyed glance. "Yeah. We're meeting in half an hour outside Billingsly's Bed and Breakfast. Why? Do you want me to go with you to meet Mrs. Thompson?"

No, I needed to show him I could work with clients all on my own. My question was leading down a different path.

"And afterward…?"

He slowly shook his head. "I'm coming back here to work on a repossession case?"

Lord, the man was dense sometimes. "Isn't Daisy meeting you at the B&B? To film that last scene?"

He flushed. "Yes, she is. It won't take long, though. Just twenty minutes at the most. She's got to be back at work, so it's not like I can take her out for brunch or anything."

I pulled a little package out of my purse and held it out to him. "You can thank me later."

He took the package with a puzzled frown and opened it, holding up the coffee mug with a colorful series of dancing cats on it. A paper fluttered to the ground.

"Make sure you pick that up and include it," I told him.

J.T. picked up the paper and read it. "Thank you for your support. One hundred percent of the profits from this purchase go to benefit Milford Mittens Cat Rescue and Foster Care."

"You're welcome."

He grinned, his face still flushed. "Did she tell you about last night?"

"Let's just say that my friend really enjoyed herself, and I expect to be reimbursed for the mug." I'd bought it for myself, but realized this morning before I left for work that it would make a wonderful after-the-first-kiss present from my boss to Daisy.

He tucked the paper inside the mug and wrapped it in the tissue once more, carefully tucking it inside his briefcase. "Well, I need to run, or I'll be late. And you as well."

I watched him leave, then quickly sorted through my papers, electing to take only my purse and a notepad as I dashed out to meet Marissa Thompson for coffee and an update on her case.

There was no need to rush, because Marissa Thompson was evidently one of those people who would probably be late to her own funeral. I was halfway through my skim latte and contemplating the professionalism of watching cat videos on my phone as I waited when she finally walked through the door. I had to wait another five minutes while she ordered her overly complicated drink, and they made it. Finally, she walked over to me like she was a model on the runway in Cannes, her drink in one hand, and her designer purse in the crook of her other arm. My irritation faded when she sat down and took off her glasses and I saw clear evidence that she'd been crying.

Professional. Must be professional. Which wouldn't involve giving our client a hug. No. Not at all.

"I'm afraid I don't have too much news to give you yet, Mrs. Thompson," I said in my kindest voice. Then I went on to outline everything I'd done so far, what I'd discovered, and what my next steps were as she listened in silence.

"Thank you."

I waited, but that was her only response.

"Are you okay?" I resisted the urge to reach out and touch her arm.

She nodded. "It's just…. Maybe I'm doing the wrong thing. Maybe I shouldn't be divorcing Spence. I loved him. I still love him."

I took a deep breath, wishing that J.T. had given me some guidance on how to handle this particular situation. Unfortunately, all I had to go on was my own sympathy for someone who was clearly going through a marital crisis.

"If you still love him, if you think there's something worth saving in your marriage, then talk to your husband," I urged her. "I've found nothing so far to indicate that he might be having an affair, and you said that was your main concern. Talk to him. Maybe the two of you could try counseling or something."

She dabbed carefully under her eyes with a napkin. "Another woman would be unforgivable, but there are things about Spencer I blindly ignored when we got married. I loved him, and just pretended those aspects of his personality didn't exist. I fooled myself into thinking that his ambition and drive were admirable career traits, but in reality, I think they're all consuming. Over the last five years I've seen Spencer become obsessed with making money. So obsessed that I think he might do something illegal or unethical if he thought it would make him rich."

I sucked in a breath. "Is that why you're looking for hidden assets? Do you think maybe he's running a scam or embezzling, or something like that?"

Marissa shook her head. "I don't have any proof of that, but Spencer has grown distant the last few years. He's distracted. And I'm pretty sure it's not his job at Fullbright and Mason, either. It's either another woman, or he's got some money-making scheme, and I'm not seeing any huge deposits into our checking accounts."

"Have you talked to him?" I asked, because if Eli had acted this way toward me, we would have been sitting down at the kitchen table for a long chat.

"Not about another woman. That would just make me look desperate. I did mention to him that he seemed to be working lots of odd hours and never had time to go to dinner or do anything with our friends, and he blew up at me. He accused me of nagging him and not being supportive of his career goals. After that, I didn't bring it up again."

"What exactly do you want to happen here, Mrs. Thompson?" I asked, again in my most gentle voice.

Her laugh was sharp with bitterness. "I'd like to go back to blissful ignorance, to a time where Spence and I went to dinner with friends, or to the club, or dancing. But that's not going to happen, so instead I want to know what's going on. I want to know if he has a mistress or is doing something illegal. If he's gambling or has some side thing going on that he's keeping from me."

"And if he does?" I asked.

Her mouth hardened into a grim line. "Then I'm going to take that bastard for every cent I can."

CHAPTER 5

*V*iolet sighed and stretched, shuffling the papers on her lap and setting them beside the tablet she'd been typing away at.

"Find anything?" I asked, looking up from my own stack of bank and credit card statements. We had taken over the entire dining room table, banishing Judge Beck to his room tonight. I'd made pork chops and roasted brussel sprouts for dinner tonight and invited the girl to join us as an added bonus to the fifty dollars I'd promised her. Madison had been thrilled, asking Violet all about her job as well as how Peony was doing at the detention center. That had made for a somewhat awkward dinner. Violet's younger sister had finally gotten her plea deal, but it hadn't been what she, and I, had been hoping for. The girl would spend the next year at the detention center, missing her entire junior year of high school. I guess it was better than being tried as an adult for second degree murder, though.

"I might have found something." Violet shuffled through the papers and handed one to me. "There's this. The abbreviation is for a property tax payment, but the amount is way less than what the tax is on the Thompsons' McMansion in Pinedale. That's paid in full through their mortgage escrow, so what got taken out of their checking account isn't a partial payment. I suspect it's not on their primary residence, but on another property."

I frowned. "He bought a house on the side?"

"Maybe. I tried to trace the reference number on the bank statement, but it's not coming up. I can't find him listed as the owner on any other properties, so either he bought them under an LLC or he's paying someone else's property taxes. We get that sometimes, especially with elderly parents."

I made a quick note—check family's real estate in county, check business entities and LLCs in state with Spencer as a forming party.

"Is there any other way to track it down?" I asked. "Like searching by the amount? Will it narrow down a list of properties and owners if we do that?"

"Not really. Sometimes people pay the annual amount, and sometimes they pay quarterly or bi-annually. If I search county property tax by annual, bi-annual, and quarterly, that's going to end up being a huge list to wade through."

I tapped my pen against my lips. "Assuming it's not a family member he's helping out, and he decided to buy something either for rentals or for a mistress, where in the heck would he get the money for a down payment? And how is he making the mortgage payments?" I held up a page of the bank statements. "That two-hundred-dollar difference in his paycheck isn't enough to cover a mortgage, and I'm not seeing anything on here besides the payments for the property he owns with his wife."

"If he bought it outright, then there wouldn't be an escrow for taxes and insurance," Violet offered. "He'd need to pay that himself each year."

I snorted. "I can't see where he had the money for a down payment, let alone buying something outright."

"You'd be surprised. Elderly people who don't have close family forget to pay their taxes or mortgage, or they have a medical emergency and can no longer afford the house. I've seen homes get snatched up for a few thousand because the ninety-year-old widow living there can't afford both her prescription medicines and the tiny mortgage payment. People fall behind, and the next thing they know, the property is at a tax or foreclosure auction."

Now *that* made me mad. "Isn't there some sort of charity that can jump in and help?" I asked, outraged at the thought of some ninety-year-old widow being evicted because she couldn't pay the measly two grand left on her mortgage.

"Yeah, but they need to apply for it. They need to speak up. It's not a common thing," she told me, "but it does happen sometimes. If it's a property tax problem and they're elderly, the county has programs available. We also refer people to Humble House. It's a non-profit foundation that buys out people's mortgages. It's kind of a reverse mortgage deal from what I've seen."

I took a breath. "Okay, so we're thinking that this guy siphoned eight or nine thousand from his paycheck into some secret savings account, then bought a house on the cheap at auction?"

"It could be. The tax payment was three months ago." Violet looked up. "You know, this 'savings plan' could have started five years ago, and the two-hundred-dollar difference you noted is an increase from what he'd been siphoning off before. If that's the case, he could have accumulated twenty or thirty thousand. That's definitely enough to pick up a distressed property at a tax or foreclosure sale."

I was ready to pull my hair out over this. "How far do I

seriously need to go back on this?" I asked her, already wondering how I was going to spin this to Marissa.

"Five, ten years?" She shrugged. "Ask the wife. They usually have a good nose for when this sort of thing started. I know my mom can pinpoint to the day when dad starts drinking or gambling again."

"She said things started going bad about five years ago." I rubbed between my eyebrows at the headache that was threatening to form. "So, twenty grand would buy him a house? Then what? He'd have rental income and a property to manage? Seems like a lot of work for very little gain, if you ask me."

Violet shrugged again. "Maybe he's one of those flippers."

"Pardon?" I was envisioning the dolphin from that show I'd watched as a kid.

"Flippers. Or tax lien sharks. Either one."

"I have no idea what either of those things mean," I told the girl.

"They're get-rich-quick schemes. It was a lot more popular about ten years back. People would buy up houses at tax and foreclosure auctions super cheap, throw a few thousand into some cosmetic repairs, then sell them for a big profit. Back when the market crashed, sometimes a house would be underwater, and the lender would retain the title at the auction because it was worth more on their books than they could get on the market. The balance sheet can only take so many hits, you know? So, if they couldn't buy something cheap enough at foreclosure auction to flip, then these get-rich folks would haunt the tax sales instead. Mortgage companies are swamped and can't always keep up. Sometimes back taxes slip through the cracks and if some enterprising person buys the tax lien, they can basically hold the mortgage company hostage for double or triple what they paid. House can't be sold until someone pays off the lien, so it's really just a waiting game."

"English please," I teased. "I never learned accountant-speak in college, but I'm a former journalist. I learn fast."

She laughed. "Okay. There are a few ways people lose their homes. Most of the time it's due to job loss or unexpected medical costs or some family crisis. The family sometimes knows it's coming. They put their house on the market and sell it fast. The mortgage bankers work with them because companies really don't want to have to go through the expense of foreclosing on a house, and they really don't want to own it and deal with the upkeep or the sale, all while it's vacant and getting trashed by neighborhood kids."

"Got it."

"Now that doesn't work when there's a housing slump, like the crash ten years ago. Suddenly people need to unload their homes, and they can't because that twenty-percent equity they had is gone. Sometimes the house is worth fifty or sixty thousand less than the mortgage. That's when it goes to auction and in those cases, the lender winds up holding the bag."

"Because the mortgage company doesn't want to sell it for too far under what they have invested in the house. And a private investor can't buy it cheap enough to make any money on the resale."

"Exactly. The lender is willing to lose a good bit, especially in a crash, because they don't want to have to manage thousands of properties that can't sell for any more than half the lien amount. They'll take the loss at auction at close to fair market value, but not at flipper prices."

This was fascinating. I pushed the papers aside and leaned over the table. "Go on."

"There are those cases like I said, where someone is elderly and doesn't owe much on their mortgage, but just can't pay it. Those are the houses flippers snatch up at auction for ten or twenty thousand. That and they like to read the obituaries and approach people who inherited houses as part of an estate. Lots of times those people just want to unload the house for as little time and effort as possible. The flipper gets a lowball appraisal, offers eighty-percent cash at closing, then flips the property."

"Eighty percent?" I wrinkled my nose. "That doesn't leave much profit, does it?"

"It's all in the appraisal," Violet told me. "They vary. And people that inherit aren't always that savvy about local markets. Paying eighty percent of a low appraisal is some-times like paying fifty percent of a fair appraisal."

I suddenly pictured Spencer Thompson at all those county events, schmoozing with real estate professionals. I was willing to bet a lot of those people he was sharing drinks with in those pictures were appraisers.

"Go on. You mentioned tax sales as well?"

"Yep. Some flippers like to also haunt the tax sales, then basically blackmail the lender or the owner double or triple the tax lien price, making their money that way. It's not really flipping, but it can be a lucrative source of money."

Flipping and tax lien scams. It was a whole world I'd been completely unaware of. It made sense based on the company Spencer Thompson seemed to keep. And the mysterious tax payment from his checking account seemed to fit in with that scenario as well.

"Do you have a way of tracking those people who buy at tax and foreclosure auctions?" I asked. "I mean, without crossing the line at work?"

She smiled. "Of course. All that is public record. Do you want me to pull a list of all non-property owners who have paid the tax lien at auction in the last five years? And what houses were sold at foreclosure auctions?"

I thought about that for a moment. Spencer was probably using an LLC or shell company for this, but I might be able to connect a name or two with what I hoped to dig up at the State Licensing Division.

"Yes, please. And I probably owe you more than fifty dollars at this point."

She waved the comment away. "This is the sort of thing I really want to do for a career. The county tax office is just a stepping stone. Your company name on my resume, plus a reference is worth the extra work."

"You do realize that ninety percent of forensic accounting is probably high-profile divorce cases like this one," I warned her.

"Yes, but there's a lot of bank fraud and corporate embezzlement, too. I wouldn't even mind leveraging my county job for a federal one. My major was accounting, but I minored in IT security, and I'm taking some online Master's classes to get an advanced degree."

She was so driven and focused. And I couldn't help but compare her to her sisters—especially Peony.

"What...what spurred this interest of yours?" I asked, trying not to insult the girl.

She flushed. "You mean a poor girl from the 'hood getting into accounting and cyber security?"

"I'm sorry—"

"It's okay, honestly. Lots of kids from the wrong end of town go into law enforcement, trying to make a difference. This is my way of making a difference. I grew up with crime, but it was the sort of stuff that's stereotypical for a poor neighborhood. Smash and grab. Dime bag deals. Two-bit cons. Like when we were in middle school and we needed to have a tablet for schoolwork. The rich kids got theirs new from their parents. The middle-income kids had the rental tablets from the school system. For the poor kids, you needed a form filled out by your parents, and they'd waive the rental fee."

I nodded, wondering where she was going with this.

"The only problem is some kids couldn't get their parents to sign. Maybe they were embarrassed, or maybe too drunk to sign it. Most of us just forged our parents' signatures. Some kids went out and stole a tablet from somewhere and used that. Some just went without and failed."

"I'm assuming you just forged your mom's signature?" I asked, knowing Violet wouldn't have jeopardized her future by committing robbery.

"Yeah, on that as well as all my financial aid forms for college. But there was a kid who hacked into the school system. If you paid him a few bucks, he'd get you the tablet, or two or three. He'd change grades. He'd make it look like kids had paid the fees for sports, even though they hadn't. And he wouldn't do it for the rich kids, either, only us poor ones. We all kept mum about it, and no one ever knew. He's probably still doing it."

I frowned. "Your grades...?"

She blushed. "I earned mine, but there were lots of football kids who didn't earn those Cs that kept them on the team."

"Holt?" I asked.

Her smile was full of fond nostalgia. "I don't speak ill of the dead. Anyway, I knew that hacker kid. And I thought if he could do that barely knowing how to find the control-alt-delete keys, then someone with far more savvy in IT systems, or in processes and procedures for handling large sets of data, could become rich."

"Did you ever think of becoming rich that way?" I asked. "Because I'm not sure I would have blamed you for that."

"No." A dimple creased her left cheek. "Wealthy people with connected families get away with that stuff, not poor people. Besides, I don't really care about the money. I want to catch the crooks and send them to jail, especially the ones who think they're too smart to get caught. That's what drives me."

I nodded, completely understanding this young girl. "So, we've got flippers running icky but legal scams with property tax liens. What else?"

"With some of those property tax purchases, they end up with the house. Those are the cases where someone has died and the estate is in limbo or there is no immediate next of kin. Some are where an elderly person forgot their tax bill, and there isn't any family to bail them out. Sometimes it's just an abandoned house and who knows what happened to the owners. Those places aren't in the best of shape. The flippers have to basically foreclose on the house with the tax lien to get a clear title. Then they fix it up and sell it."

"Okay. That's property tax auctions. Anything else?"

"Like I said, sometimes they can do a lowball purchase of an estate property. Out-of-state grandkids, none of whom want the house and just want the whole thing settled and done so they can move on. The flipper buys it with a quick close and no inspection or repairs, and then fixes it up and sells it quick."

"Basically, buy cheap and sell for a profit." I looked down at the bank statements. "So, where do you think this guy would be getting the money for this?"

"Well, if he started siphoning money from his paycheck a decade ago and was able to pick up one or two purchases for a few thousand, he could be funding recent investments from the sales profits of those earlier homes," she suggested.

"The guy's only thirty-five. I can't imagine he's been running this thing more than five years without his wife knowing. Plus, ten years ago she would have noticed hundreds of dollars a week coming out of his paycheck. He wasn't making the big bucks then to hide it. Plus, plus, I can't see this guy stashing money for ten years, saving up for this business. I get the impression it's a strike-while-the-iron-is-hot scheme, and I don't think this man has the patience to wait very long before beginning to run his side gig."

Violet tilted her head. "So, you've met him? The husband, I mean?"

"No. I probably should, though." Why hadn't I thought of that before? I knew from back in my newspaper days that there was a lot you could glean from a face-to-face conversation. I didn't have to make this an interview or pump him for information, just get a read on who Spencer Thompson was as a person.

It seemed like tomorrow would be a good time to talk to someone about estate planning.

CHAPTER 6

$\mathcal{O}$ne of the best things about having my private investigator's license was not having to be in the office at eight thirty each morning. J.T. did prefer I spent as much time as possible actually working from the office so I could meet with any clients that happened to walk through the door, as well as receive couriered packages and phone calls from our skip trace clients, but he understood that there was a certain amount of feet-on-the-street my new position required.

I called and managed to get an appointment with Spencer Thompson without much trouble. They fit me in for Thursday, and then I called Mrs. Thompson and updated her with my progress.

By the time I rolled into the office, it was close to noon. J.T. was nowhere to be found, but he'd left me a full pot of coffee that seemed reasonably fresh. He'd also left me a note that there was a turkey and Havarti on rye in the fridge for me. I was thrilled, and not just because I loved turkey and Havarti on rye, but because the sandwich was my boss's way of telling me I was doing a great job. That, and a not-so-subtle hint that he wanted me to work through lunch.

I'd planned to do so anyway, so I unpacked my laptop, pulled the sandwich from the fridge, and got cracking.

There were tens of thousands of DBAs, sole proprietorships, and LLCs formed in the county within the last five years. I picked five years since that's when Marissa Thompson said things in their marriage started to change. Five years gave me what I hoped would be an adequate buffer for Spencer to get funding and get things set up. There was always a chance he'd started before that, but Spencer Thompson was young, and he didn't begin work for Fullbright and Mason until five years ago. I figured that before he'd started at the investment company, not only did he not have enough money to start a side business, but he was probably focused on his primary career instead.

Looking at the huge file of business names, I immediately discarded all the restaurants, dry cleaners, nail salons, and bakeries as well as other retail brick-and-mortar establishments, figuring that Spencer Thompson wouldn't be able to run that sort of business on the side without his wife knowing about it. I doubted any of those would have appealed to him as a passive investment either, given when I knew about their high rate of failure and miserable early profit margins.

That still left me with nearly four thousand businesses to look through. I ate my sandwich and thought about what Violet had said, deciding to start with those whose purpose involved real estate or finance. Now I was down to two hundred.

None of the DBA businesses were listed as having an S. Thompson as an owner, but one LLC had him as a partner—Humble Properties, LLC.

Humble Properties. I frowned, trying to remember where

I'd heard that name before. Thankfully, a quick Google search enlightened me. There was a non-profit foundation named Humble House, and Humble Properties, LLC—which looked to be very much the sort of thing Violet would call a "flipper" company.

But the non-profit...It was the foundation Violet had said they sometimes referred elderly homeowners to. I scrolled through their website, seeing that they offered free consultations, a Medicaid application service, and a reverse-mortgage service, where the homeowner could receive a lump sum, a line of credit, or monthly payments from the equity on their home with no need to repay until they moved or died. The foundation also offered a special program where the homeowner would deed the property to the foundation in return for a monthly stipend. They were allowed to live in their home payment-free until their demise, and at that time, the home would become the property of Humble House.

Humble Properties, LLC, on the other hand, bought distressed properties, improved them, then sold them. Completely different missions. The only thing in common between the two companies was the similar name.

That and one of the owners—someone by the name of Tracey Abramson.

It made me wonder what that non-profit did when they ended up owning a house. I was pretty sure that the home would quickly be transferred to the for-profit entity which would fix it up and sell it. I did a quick calculation in my head and realized that if the non-profit were savvy about life expectancy as well as careful on how much they needed to spend, they could turn a tidy profit in their special program deals. For a three-hundred-thousand-dollar value house, they could pay off an existing mortgage, fork out the taxes and insurance, and pay the homeowner a monthly stipend, and when the elderly owner passed in ten years, they'd be owners of a home with a hundred and thirty thousand dollar profit plus appreciation.

Of course, it would be a long game. There might be a time or two when someone died within a year or so after signing the contract, but the majority of their investment probably wouldn't be recouped for a decade or maybe two. All of that meant there needed to be a whole lot of cash for the initial outlay. Or a good relationship with some subprime lenders, if the numbers allowed.

Or possibly a for-profit entity that provided enough money to allow the owners to play the long game with the allegedly non-profit business.

Maybe I was being cynical. All of this seemed above board, and I had no idea what the relationship between the foundation and the LLC were, nor what kind of business dealings these two had in common. For all I knew, the for-profit company was funding the foundation for a tax write-off and some community good will. It could be entirely legitimate.

But then why was Spencer Thompson listed as a partner on the LLC, and why had he never told his wife about it?

I wasn't sure what sort of assets there would be for Marissa to take in a divorce, but she definitely needed to know that her husband had a share in this business. I looked again at the social media posts and pictures, all with Spencer Thompson rubbing elbows with the movers and shakers of real estate and mortgage banking in the county. There wasn't much on the Humble House's for-profit company. No website other than a one--page summary with some generic contact form. But clearly Spencer Thompson was listed as a partner in this business with Tracey Abramson.

Tracy. I frowned, remembering that Marissa had said her husband had made several clandestine phone calls and that name had come up. I'd assumed, as she'd obviously done, that

Tracy was a woman, but the spelling with the "e" usually was for a man. I searched Tracey Abramson on the internet, and sure enough, came up with all sorts of social media for a man of that name in Milford. He appeared to be about my age, had left a top-level position with a national lender, and formed his non-profit locally. The pictures showed a portly bald man with a broad grin, friendly blue eyes, and a flair for well-tailored suits. I recognized a few of the charity functions he and his wife attended as ones that Matt Poffenberger had put on. I admired the nice boat they had docked at their lake house in a few of the photos. Then I saw it—the picture that I'd been looking for.

Tracey Abramson at a Chamber of Commerce event two years ago, standing arm-in-arm with Spencer Thompson.

CHAPTER 7

racey Abramson was shockingly easy to locate through his foundation's website contact information, and even easier to meet with. No appointment necessary. I just showed up at the Humble House office, told the receptionist that I was soliciting hole sponsors and players for the October Fill the Food Bank charity golf tourney, and that Matt Poffenberger had asked me to inquire if Mr. Abramson would be interested in partnering in a spring fundraiser. I got right in the door, and I didn't really feel that guilty about dropping Matt's name. I did still have two holes that needed sponsors for the tourney, and I knew he could always use an extra team as well as fundraising partners.

One thing was clear upon entering Mr. Abramson's office —he might be running a non-profit foundation, but he was very, very rich. The wood floors looked like they'd been lifted from a centuries-old barn and lovingly restored. A faded oriental rug sat in front of the desk, clearly something that should have belonged in a museum. High quality original art and sculpture decorated the room, and the centerpiece of the room, the desk, was hand-carved mahogany. I immediately thought of what fun Henry would have here with all the antiquities.

The man behind the desk was no less impressive. Tracey Abramson had a full head of snow-white hair, trimmed in a timeless style with a debonair curl defying the rest to hang on his forehead with disheveled grace. As he stood, his warm brown eyes danced with humor and a smile creased his handsome face. I shook his hand, thinking that Mrs. Abramson was a very lucky woman.

"Mrs. Carrera. I knew your husband, Eli. I was saddened to hear of his passing this spring. You have my deepest condolences. He was a brilliant surgeon and an asset to our community. We all feel his loss."

I thanked him, surprised to realize that I might have gotten in to see the man without an appointment on the strength of my own name, not Matt's. A lot of people had known Eli either in a professional capacity or socially. Surgeons worked insane hours, but Eli had always been able to fit in time for friends. Not that I thought Tracey Abramson was a friend of my late husband's. Clearly their relationship had either been doctor-patient, or the man before me was a significant donor at the hospital and had gotten to know Eli that way. I was banking on the latter.

"You tell Matt there's nothing he can do that will get me out on a golf course." Mr. Abramson sat back down and motioned me to do the same. "Humble House would be honored to sponsor a hole at the tourney, though. And I'd be very interested in discussing a joint fundraising project. Our elderly population is in crisis, Mrs. Carrera. Foreclosures among those over seventy are disturbingly high. People are losing their homes with no financial resources to find alternate housing, and often without any family to help them. A crisis."

I sat, the investigative journalist in me perking up her

ears. "A crisis is often another man's opportunity. Not to imply anything, Mr. Abramson, but these reverse mortgages and other programs you offer are structured to turn a profit, are they not?"

He laughed. "We're a non-profit foundation, Mrs. Carrera. Every dime we make is accounted for and needs to further our mission to help the elderly live their lives in the homes they've loved. Whether that's through a traditional reverse mortgage, or one of our other, more creative, options."

"But surely there's a profit more times than there's a loss?" I gave him my most charming smile. "You've got to keep the lights on here. I'm genuinely curious. How do you structure these programs so you're not taking a bath on every one of them?"

"There is a lot of risk," he admitted. "But as a non-profit foundation, we can afford to take chances that banks and other for-profit financial entities can't. Sometimes we'll take a loss, and sometimes we'll turn a profit. All that matters is that we work toward our mission of helping the elderly."

"But there's a for-profit entity you own as well," I pointed out. "In cases where you have the title, Humble House sells the house to them. They do repairs and sell it without the same restrictions this business would have as a 501c3."

Tracey Abramson laughed again but shifted uncomfortably in his chair. "Is this extortion for me to sponsor an additional hole? Or for me to get out there and make an absolute fool of myself on the golf course? If so, tell Matt he's failed. That's all public knowledge, and there's nothing at all shady about our business structure. The foundation simply doesn't have the resources or staff to prepare a house for sale where the LLC does. Our finances are above board and available for audit if there is any concern that we're abusing our non-profit status."

I realized immediately that I'd approached this wrong. I didn't want to offend the man, especially since he knew Matt so well and clearly had known my husband. I backpedaled and stuck the bristling investigative journalist back in the box, trying to approach this as a budding detective and part-time charity fundraiser.

"I'm sorry. I didn't mean to insinuate that you were doing anything unethical here. It's just that I've never come across this kind of foundation before and I'm curious about how you're structured and how you managed to set it all up. What made you decide to start Humble House? Why the elderly, and housing in particular?" I smiled. "Clearly someone doesn't start a non-profit for the money. Was there a personal reason you made this your focus?"

He relaxed, leaning back in his chair. "Growing up in money doesn't mean you have to be blind to the plight of others. Back when I was a boy, it wasn't unusual to go over to a friend's house and see their grandparents or great aunts and uncles living with them—rich, middle-class, poor, it didn't matter. Children took care of their elderly. But now… So many people didn't have children, or have outlived them, or their sons and daughters aren't in a position to help them. Every day I see men and women in the golden years of their lives, not wanting to bother their busy children with their troubles, not wanting the humiliation of asking them for help. People want to be independent until their last day. They want to stay in the homes they've lived in most of their adult life. They don't want to be a burden. Helping the elderly retain some dignity late in life by being able to stay in their homes and having some additional income is my passion, Mrs. Carrera. When I started Humble House thirty years ago, we mainly offered free financial advice to the elderly and assistance in filing for Medicaid and other assistance programs. Now, I'm proud to be able to offer reverse mortgages and other home equity programs as part of our mission. But with those more complex programs came more complex management issues involving what to do with the properties when the client passed on and we took possession of the home."

I'd come in here thinking this was a money-making scam, but the longer I spoke with this man, the more I believed he was truly trying to help people. Was this what had Spencer Thompson so distracted the last five years? Was this what he was keeping from his wife? She'd thought he was cheating on her, or running a swindle for financial gain, and instead he was spending his time working for a noble cause?

"Tell me how these special programs work," I said, intrigued by the whole thing. "You offer something that sounds like a reverse mortgage in exchange for the unencumbered title on the house?"

He nodded. "Reverse mortgages are a federal program, but for those who want something different, we have what we call the Humble House Delayed Buyout, or HHDB. In that program, we have actuaries run the numbers, pay off any existing mortgages and tax liens, and assume all financial responsibility for the house, including repair and upkeep. We do a walk through every year, just to ensure there are no significant repairs needed, and we pay all taxes and insurance. The owner receives a monthly stipend which continues until they pass on, whether or not they live in the home until they die or transition into an assisted-living facility. At that time, we assume possession of the home, giving the family a month to remove any belongings they want to retain."

It did sound like a good program. The owner would stay in their home without worry of upkeep, paying mortgage, or property taxes. They'd get a nice little monthly income for the rest of their life. True, there wouldn't be a home to pass on to their heirs, but how many people's children actually wanted their parents' house anyway? I didn't know the numbers, but I was pretty sure most of those houses got sold after the owners passed away.

"Are there ever any issues with clearing belongings out of the home?" I asked. "My across-the-street neighbor just passed four months ago, and his nephew is *still* sorting through all his things."

"We do try to be understanding and work with the family. Generally, we can offer a short-term rent-back as a low monthly fee if they need more than thirty days to resolve the estate." He shrugged. "Sometimes a lot gets left behind and we contract with a company to go in and clear it all out for us. Well, the LLC does. Again, that sort of thing isn't our area of expertise. When we started offering these home equity programs, we weren't really prepared to handle the mechanics of turning a house around for sale. It made sense to start another company to do just that and leave us to manage our programs and outreach."

Tracey Abramson sounded like a good man. He definitely balanced his charitable instincts with good business savvy, but that was needed in today's world if he expected this non-profit to survive to help people beyond a few decades. But as saintly as this all sounded, there still was that for-profit side company to figure into the equation. And there was still Spencer Thompson's role to figure out.

"The goal at Humble House is not to lose money, but to make enough that we can expand into things like meal deliveries, assistance to those who needed help with medical bills or nursing home costs, or even funeral expenses for a spouse," Mr. Abramson continued. "Honestly, I thought that selling the properties to a side enterprise that wasn't as encumbered would be a wise idea, so five years ago I established Humble Properties, LLC with someone who had experience in turning around homes for sale."

"A partner?" I tried to act as though I didn't already know this. "How is that working out?"

A spark of something that looked like anger lit up his eyes. "Partnerships can be a rocky road. This past year, I've realized that wasn't the direction I wanted to go. I'm working to buy out my partner and shut down that business. Going forward, I plan to have that managed through Humble House in a very different fashion."

I was amazed that he'd been so forthcoming. But now came the question that might get me thrown out of his office, widow of a notable surgeon or not. "And your partner in this for-profit side company was Spencer Thompson at Full-bright and Mason? What exactly is his role in the LLC, and how much did he put into the startup of this joint business venture?"

Tracey Abramson went very still, then leaned forward, resting his hands on the top of his expensive desk. "And what would that have to do with the charity golf tournament or your curiosity about the workings of a non-profit foundation?"

Crap. I felt like I was playing chess with a master, carefully maneuvering my pieces and trying not to get my king trapped in a corner. "In my day job, I work for Pierson Investigative and Recovery Services, Mr. Abramson. Yes, I'm here to gain your support for the charity golf tournament, but there's another reason that I'm here. I can't tell you the exact nature of that other reason, but please know that my question has everything to do with Spencer Thompson, and not you or your business."

This wasn't a criminal investigation. I wasn't the police, or the IRS, or even an investigative journalist anymore. I was simply a detective, trying to see if Spencer Thompson was hiding money from his soon-to-be-ex-wife.

Tracey Abramson eyed me steadily for a moment. "I don't

want trouble for Humble House. I've had a spotless career, and my family name is unblemished. I want this non-profit foundation to be my legacy, and I don't want it tainted by any hint of scandal."

I held my breath. "I understand. I only want to know what part Spencer Thompson played, and what, if any, profit he may have made from either his work as a partner of Humble Properties, LLC or any other company you might be aware of."

Mr. Abramson let out a breath and shook his head. "I knew that man was too slick for his own good. What has he gotten himself into? No, don't answer that." He waved a hand. "I don't want to know the details."

"I really don't want to cause you or Humble House any problems, Mr. Abramson," I told him. "I was speaking with someone with the county tax assessor's office the other day who spoke quite highly of the service your non-profit offers. Honestly, I only want to know about your dealings with Spencer Thompson. That and to secure your sponsorship for the charity golf tournament."

He shot me a wry smile. "You remind me of my sister. Shrewd and not a woman to be at cross purposes with. Your husband was a lucky man, Mrs. Carrera. Yes, you have my sponsorship. As for Spencer Thompson…"

I waited patiently for him to gather his thoughts and continue.

"Fullbright and Mason is a blue-chip financial services firm. My father used them. Heck, I think my grandfather probably used them. I've set up a few non-revocable trust funds with their assistance, as well as transferred the management of my investments to them. When I decided thirty years ago to establish Humble House, I consulted with a few of their partners on issues involving the elderly, thinking the insight might help me in forming my company.

I've maintained close ties with them, and through various activities in the county."

"When did you first meet Spencer Thompson?" I pressed.

"Five years ago, when he was just starting out at Full-bright and Mason. He was bold, but knowledgeable, and I was impressed. I ran into him at a Chamber event and probably had a glass too many when I began to talk to him about some properties we'd recently acquired and how I was struggling with the decision of what to do with them."

"He does specialize in estate planning and retirement investments," I commented. "It's not unusual that you'd confide in him or seek his advice. He seems to be well respected, and knowledgeable in his field, and he does have a position at a prestigious investment firm."

Mr. Abramson shrugged. "Still, I blame the wine. Spencer is a savvy businessman, though. He laid out a plan to establish a for-profit arm of the foundation and sell these troublesome properties there as distressed assets. The LLC would manage fixing up the house, then selling the properties at a fair market value. Initially we'd start with the properties sold to the LLC by Humble House, but then expand into flipping other distressed homes around the county. I took a chance and Thompson and I began a joint business venture together."

"One that you said you're in the process of dissolving?"

He grimaced. "Yes. Early on it became clear that Spencer and I had very different visions for the future of the company. I began to feel uncomfortable with some of his tactics. They were completely legal, but in my opinion, they seemed to be taking advantage of the very people I'd established Humble House to protect. We had words. We had words over several years, then last winter I informed Spencer that I intended to dissolve the business. We've been at a bit of a stalemate since then. He's offered to run it with me as a silent partner, but I'm not sure I want to continue to do business with that man in any capacity. Last week I received an offer from him to buy me out."

Buy him out? My mouth nearly hit the floor in shock. Where had he gotten the money? Had he been flipping properties on the side as well as for this business? Was there something illegal going on as his wife feared? His expertise had no doubt played a role in getting the initial partnership with Tracey Abramson, but where was he coming up with the funds to buy out half the business?

Follow the money. It's what Violet would have said, and I agreed. Where the heck did Spencer get the cash to do all this?

"If you don't mind my asking, what exactly went wrong between you two?" I asked. "I know you said a philosophical difference?"

Mr. Abramson hesitated, then sighed. "Off the record? The Humble House transfers were going well, but the issues came in when Humble Properties began to start flipping properties outside of the foundation. Spencer wanted to grab up houses at tax sales. There was one house in particular where I felt the company was taking advantage of an elderly homeowner who quite possibly didn't have the mental faculties to know he'd missed his payments. In my eyes, the man needed assistance, and I wanted to offer him help through Humble House. Spencer insisted we buy the house at auction, evict the man, and flip the property for a profit. It didn't sit well with me, and I was gravely concerned that such actions would taint the reputation of my foundation. It was one of many ethical differences we had between us. I began to worry that Spencer's methods were more about making money in any way possible, and that eventually his business practices were going to harm both mine and my foundation's reputation. I'll be happy when this LLC is dissolved and I can put this whole business behind me. And I'll be quite happy to never see Spencer Thompson again."

"I appreciate this, Mr. Abramson," I told him. "If there's anything else you know, I'd be very appreciative if you gave me a call." I dug out a business card and handed it to him. He took it and read it with a smirk.

"Pierson, huh? I'd figured you for the socialite housewife of a surgeon, not a private investigator."

It was my turn to smirk. "I was an investigative journalist when I met Eli, and throughout our marriage until his accident. It's not a big leap from that to private investigations."

He nodded. "I underestimated you, Mrs. Carrera. Please make sure to mark us down for our hole sponsorship and tell Matt to give me a call about this spring."

"Thank you for your time, and for your sponsorship, Mr. Abramson," I said as I got to my feet. Halfway toward the door, he called out to me.

"Oh, and Mrs. Carrera? You might to look into a little company called Brockhurst Properties. I know I am."

I gave him a nod, and a quick smile, then headed out, thinking there was more to Spencer Thompson than I'd originally thought.

CHAPTER 8

*B*rockhurst Properties wasn't easy to find. They had no social media presence, nothing registered with the state as far as a licensed business entity. A broad credit check came up with seventy listings with the same or similar names, none of them in the state. On a hunch I called Violet, hoping it was okay for her to take a somewhat personal call at work.

"Oh, I've been meaning to call you," she exclaimed the moment she answered her phone. "I probably shouldn't have done this, but I went into the county accounting system and looked up transactions the week of that property tax payment. I matched up the transaction numbers and found the property."

I caught my breath, happy to finally have a lead in a whole lot of nothing. "Violet, you're incredible!"

"I know!" she laughed. "Four-twenty-eight Willow Drive in Marshall Heights."

Marshall Heights. That was a tiny one-street town east of Locust Point. There were lots of 1960s bungalow-style homes from what I could recall, and a whole lot of residents who'd bought them when they were brand spanking new. Other than a gas station and a pizza parlor, the town was strictly residential.

"Who owns the house?" I asked.

"A Brockhurst Properties."

I barely had time to process that before she continued.

"They picked it up at a foreclosure sale about nine months ago and it looks like they're winding down an eviction of the former owner. No doubt they'll slap a fresh coat of paint on it and have it sold in six months."

Flippers. Just as she'd predicted yesterday. Just as Tracey Abramson had alluded. Spencer Thompson was a flipper with not just one, but two businesses on the side. But where the heck was he getting the money for this?

"How much did it go for at the foreclosure sale?" I asked. He'd probably stashed whatever he'd made at Humble Properties, LLC in a separate account that I'd yet to find, but how much had that amounted to over the last five years? Enough to fund the startup-up of this new business? And how the heck was he not including that income on his tax returns?

"Brockhurst Properties bought it for fifty thousand. The tax assessment value of the house is one hundred and thirty. It looks like the foreclosure was on a lien of one hundred thousand." She caught her breath. "Oh. This is sad."

"What?" I was practically on the edge of my seat. Who knew that accounting and mortgages could be so intriguing?

"The former owner, a man with the unfortunate name of Melvin Elmer, took the loan a year ago. He never paid on it. He's the original owner of the house when it was built in 1962, so he's got to be in his eighties or even nineties."

"So, this Mr. Elmer took out a hundred-thousand-dollar loan on a house, but never made one payment? What did he use the money for?"

"Beat's me." I heard the clacking of Violet's keyboard in

the background. "Maybe medical expenses? Although I can't imagine what crazy treatment would have cost that and not been covered by Medicare. Maybe he has a gambling habit. Maybe he has a son with a gambling habit who was about to be fitted with cement shoes."

Maybe Violet had been watching too many gangster movies lately.

"He paid off the house fifteen years ago by the lien release on file," she continued. "This poor man. I hope he has somewhere to go because the eviction is in a week."

"Thanks, Violet." I almost hung up before I remembered the reason I'd called her. "Oh! Actually, I was calling to ask you about Brockhurst Properties, ironically enough. Can you check and see if they own any other properties in the county?"

"On it," she told me.

I hung up and settled in to search for anything I could find on Melvin Elmer. He had a rather barren credit report aside from the glaring foreclosure. Not much in the way of assets as far as I could tell. There was a tiny pension from the railroad, but it looked like the majority of his income was from his Social Security paycheck. The house loan was at a higher than expected interest rate, no doubt due to his low income and lack of recent credit. Looking at the monthly payment amount, I was surprised it had gone into foreclosure. It would have been tight, but Mr. Elmer should have been able to squeeze that into his budget.

But he hadn't made one payment. Not one. The foreclosure proceedings had gone through with lightning speed, and seemingly no protest at all by the homeowner from the notes on the judicial case search site.

I picked up the phone and grimaced, realizing that I might be in for another late night. Sheesh, I was getting to be worse than Judge Beck on a non-custody week. Tracey

Abramson had already left for the day, but his receptionist kindly took a message and promised to deliver it first thing in the morning. I hung up the phone and with another glance at the clock, gathered my things to take a drive out to Marshall Heights.

* * *

I PARKED along the curb in front of 428 Willow Drive and sat in the car for a few seconds, checking to make sure I'd written down the correct address. I'd expected a home in disrepair with an overgrown lawn and scraggly hedges. Instead I was looking at a neat one-story with lush, recently mown grass and a line of boxwoods that looked like they'd been trimmed with the use of a level. Softening the harsh lines of the hedge were curved beds with a wild profusion of Nippon Daisy, Joe Pye Weed, Goldenrod, and Japanese anemone. Flanking the driveway were red helenium alternating with bright orange chrysanthemum. This clearly wasn't a property in distress. Although I was no expert, I recognized a carefully maintained garden when I saw one. Anyone who took the time and care to plant these blooms would no doubt have bulbs and other flowers that would fill in these beds with completely different selection for each season. Either the owner in the recent past had enough money to afford a professional landscaper to plan and maintain this property, or they were lovingly doing it themselves. Neither option pointed toward someone who would take out nearly all the equity on their home with no ability to repay the loan even in monthly installments.

This place had been treasured. Was it a relative whose financial needs came before a beloved home? Had something suddenly, desperately come up and the home hadn't had the chance to show the neglect? Either way, it was with a heavy heart that I got out of my car and approached the front door. This was too reminiscent of my own situation—and what might be my situation if Judge Beck ended up moving out in a year or two. I'd struggled to keep my old Victorian in reasonable repair. Eli's needs had been the priority. When he'd died, I'd found myself with an empty retirement account, two mortgages, and a bank account that might have gotten me through the three to four months it would have taken to sell my home.

This could have been me.

A man who looked well over ninety answered the door, his tanned face deeply creased with wrinkles, a set of neatly shaven jowls quivering as he pursed his lips and looked me over. Finally, he lifted deep-set brown eyes to meet mine.

"Melvin Elmer?" He was like a short, hunched-over elderly bloodhound, with a tennis-ball tipped walker and a portable oxygen tank.

"Yeah?" He growled. "I've got until Monday, so unless you're here to help me move boxes, shove off."

I winced and produced a business card, which the man read a scant inch from his eyes. "I'd like to ask you some questions about the company that acquired your home, Brockhurst Properties. And I'd be happy to help you with boxes as we talk."

He snorted and pocketed the card. "Be nice if you arrested those bastards, excuse my French. Guess it's too late for that, though. And unless things have changed since I was in the working world, private investigators don't arrest anyway."

He opened the door and motioned me in while my gaze swept the room. It was a typical, cookie-cutter layout with an open pass-through window from the living room into an eat-in kitchen. Three doors lined up along a wall to my right, no doubt to the two bedrooms and one bathroom. Small.

Utilitarian. Cozy. The floors were oak with Berber area rugs in dark brown. Outside of the scant furniture, all the belongings were already in a dozen boxes scattered by the door. Whatever financial emergency had happened to Melvin Elmer, he clearly had lived a frugal and somewhat minimalist life if all his possessions fit into a dozen large-ish boxes.

The kitchen was only partially packed. He motioned me toward a pile of dishes next to a stack of old newspapers and I began to wrap as I spoke.

"I'm working for a client, and the trail I'm following led to this Brockhurst Properties. I don't know much about them except that they appear to be property flippers, buying up distressed homes and those they can purchase far below market value at tax and foreclosure sales, then fixing them up and selling them with a quick turnaround and maximum profit."

He shrugged, pulling a handful of spoons out of a drawer and rolling them in newspaper. "I don't know anything about them. All I know is I got a notice on my door last week that said I had to move out of my home, and that this Brockhurst Properties now owns it."

"The foreclosure did seem to happen pretty quickly," I told him, adding a paper-wrapped bowl to the box of plates. "Have you met anyone from Brockhurst Properties? Who was at the eviction hearing for them?"

"Didn't go to any eviction hearing." He put his hands on the arms of the walker and turned to face me. "Didn't you hear what I was saying, lady? I didn't owe any money on this place. I didn't have any loans. First I heard anything about this was that notice on my door last week."

I hesitated, because this sounded truly unbelievable. "What exactly are you saying, Mr. Elmer? That someone fraudulently took out a loan on your home?"

He turned back to the silverware drawer. "That's exactly

what I'm saying. I didn't take out any loan. I didn't get any money."

"What happened when the coupon book and the monthly mortgage bills came to your home?" I asked, not quite believing him. I'd heard plenty of identity theft, but how could a scammer have managed to take out a mortgage on someone else's home?

"If I got any mortgage bills, I probably tossed them, thinking they were junk mail. I don't have any mortgages on this house. I don't have any bills. Most of what I get in the mail is junk—people wanting to loan me a bunch of money for this or that, or sell me insurance plans, or motorized scooters, or shit like that. Excuse my French. Every day my mailbox is full of junk and I toss ninety-nine percent of it all in the trash without even opening it."

"But it would have looked like a bill," I insisted.

"You seen the things they send you? They're all stamped 'important' or 'time sensitive' or other things. You get all freaked out thinking they're from the IRS, or you got caught by a red-light camera or something, then you open it up and some idiot company you never heard of tells you they want to loan you forty-thousand dollars at a criminal interest rate. They even call you on the phone, trying to get your bank information, pretending the government is gonna take your house if you don't give them the info. Scammers everywhere. I don't answer my phone anymore unless I know the number. And I throw away all that mail."

I couldn't say I blamed him. Lots of these companies used some unscrupulous marketing techniques, and phone scams involving the elderly were at an all-time high.

"And you didn't get the notice for the foreclosure? Or the eviction hearing?" I asked, continuing my wrapping.

"No idea if I did or not. Like I said, I throw all that stuff away. And no one put anything on my door except that notice that I gotta be out of here by Monday or they're coming with a sheriff to put all my stuff on the curb."

"Can I see a copy of that notice?"

He reached over across the table and handed me a weather-stained piece of paper. It looked official to me, but I snapped a copy of it with my cell phone camera anyway, then handed it back.

"Did you call anyone to protest this? If you're the victim of identity theft, there's got to be some way you can get this all reversed."

He paused, looking out the kitchen window into a yard filled with neatly tended gardens full of herbs and wildflowers. "Called the sheriff's office, but they said I'd need to get a lawyer and protest it. One lawyer I talked to said it's too late. Foreclosure's done and this other company owns the house. It's too late to get a stay on the eviction. He said best I could do is sue the mortgage company for failure to do some diligence or something like that, but it might take three to five years, and no guarantee I'd win anything." He shook his head. "Can't afford the retainer on the lawyer anyway. Then I called some place that's supposed to help old people stay in their homes, but they told me they couldn't help me either and sent me back to that lawyer I can't afford."

I had to grit my teeth to keep my anger in check. This was *so* wrong! If what Melvin Elmer said was true, he'd been a victim of identity theft, and could hardly be held responsible. Was he supposed to monitor his credit when he had no need for any? Open what he assumed was junk mail? He was losing his home, losing everything, all due to some thieving bastard—excuse my French.

"There has to be someone that can help," I exclaimed. "Someone at the news that can run a story and pressure this Brockhurst Properties into letting you stay here until it's all sorted out. Or a lawyer who will take this on out of principle. Someone."

He turned to face me, and in spite of the stooped shoulders, I saw a spark of something in his eyes behind the tired resignation. "You think I didn't call those Brockhurst Properties people from the notice? Soon as I got off with the sheriff's office, before I went to the lawyer, I called them. Left three messages with some stupid automated service. The man that finally got back to me said he was very sorry, but that they'd bought the property at a legal foreclosure sale, and if I had concerns about the loan the bank said I'd taken out, I would need to address that with the bank. He told me he'd paid money for my house and needed to sell it as quickly as possible because of cash flow. I begged him to give me six months, then he could have the place. Even told him I'd pay him rent. He said no."

I had to take a few breaths to calm down before I could speak again. "Did you get the name of the man you spoke to from Brockhurst Properties?"

"Some Thompson guy. Stuart or Steve or something Thompson. Works at one of them investment companies and does this stuff on the side it seems."

"Spencer Thompson?"

He shrugged, then yanked a handful of forks from the drawer. "Yeah. That's him."

I looked down at my phone at the eviction notice, then quickly set a reminder to ask for the transcripts from the eviction hearing. It was too soon to have them online, but J.T. had contacts at the courthouse. They would have copies for us tomorrow if my boss turned on his charm.

Then I sent a text to Violet, asking her to pull copies of the promissory note and deed of trust for the loan, and letting her know that there could be some identity theft and fraud involved. I was outraged. I was so angry at whoever this lender was for not ensuring the person they were writing a check to was the actual owner of the home. I was outraged that a man was being forced from his home, the home he'd lived in for nearly sixty years. And I was outraged that Spencer Thompson didn't seem to have a compassionate bone in his body.

I wanted to wring the man's neck when I met with him tomorrow. Wring his neck. Or at the very least make sure his wife took him to the cleaners in this divorce.

"Do you have somewhere to go?" I asked Mr. Elmer, half afraid he'd say 'no' and I'd end up with an elderly stranger living in my house. "Friends? Family that you can move in with?"

"There's Ralph. He's a friend up the road that said I can stay with him until I get myself straightened out. Guess I might try to find an apartment to rent after that." He raised a shaky hand to wipe his eyes and my heart broke.

"An apartment isn't so bad," I told him softly, thinking about the apartments I'd contemplated moving to this spring, when it seemed I'd never be able to keep my home.

"I've lived here almost my whole adult life," he told me. "It's the gardens I'll miss the most. I wanted to die here. I wanted to at least see my spring bulbs come up one more time, to maybe sit out on the bench and smell the lilacs in bloom, feel the warm sun on my face."

I suddenly realized why he was so reluctant to fight this and sue the bank, why three to five years in a lawsuit was more a problem than the fact he might not win.

"Mr. Elmer...do you...are you...?" How do you ask if someone is dying? Especially a stranger?

He nodded. "Been fighting it for years now. A few weeks ago, the doctor told me there wasn't any more they could do. Gave me six months. All I want is to see the spring bulbs come up and smell the lilacs one more time. I begged that

81

Thompson man for six months. I begged him. I told him I wouldn't fight for the house, I wouldn't sue, that he could have it if he'd just give me until next spring."

Oh, God. Now I was the one wiping my eyes. I blinked away my tears, looking out the big window over the sink to the lovely flowers and bushes in the back yard. "Let me see what I can do, Mr. Elmer. I'm not promising anything but let me see if I can get some kind of temporary stay on the eviction, or a lawyer who might be able to help you, or…something."

"Six months," he told me before turning back to wrap the silverware in newspaper. "All I want is six months."

CHAPTER 9

I was running late due to my after-work detour to Marshall Heights, and I'd promised Judge Beck I'd make dinner, so with a creative mind I surveyed the contents of my fridge and cabinets at quarter to six that evening. I had fifteen minutes before the rest of my household got home tonight, and not a lot that I could throw together in that short a time.

"There's that leftover chicken," I announced to Taco, who looked as if he'd been hoping that leftover chicken would wind up in his bowl. "Or stuffed peppers? I don't think I can pull that off in fifteen minutes, though. Maybe a stir fry with the chicken?"

Taco agreed with a meow, and I turned to the shadow hovering by the sink. "What do you think?"

The ghost was silent, as always. In life, Eli would have most definitely have had an opinion, and that opinion probably would have involved us going out to dinner.

"Stir fry it is." I pulled the chicken out of the fridge and sat a pan on the stove, splashing a bit of olive oil on the bottom before turning the burner on. I had some vegetables from my trip to the farmer's market on Sunday, and some quinoa I could cook up instead of rice. With a spirit of improvisation, I threw everything together and was just getting the table set when Judge Beck and the kids walked through the door.

"We made it home alive!" Henry announced.

"Brat." Madison swatted her brother then plopped her backpack by the stairs. "Here, Miss Kay. I'll set the table. What's for dinner?"

"Stir fry," I announced. "Things were kind of hectic today, and I didn't have time for anything more involved."

"Sounds good to me." Henry sniffed. "Smells good to me, too."

"Help Miss Kay, then go wash up," Judge Beck told the two kids before turning to me. "Any progress on that case you were working on last night?"

My stomach knotted up as I thought once more about Melvin Elmer. "Definitely progress, but there's something I discovered that I want to ask you about later."

"Absolutely. Remember that I have a duty to report."

"If I was aware of a crime, I'd be telling the police before I told you anyway," I said, heading back into the kitchen. "This is more someone being a jerk. It's a social injustice, and I want your thoughts on options."

The judge followed me into the kitchen, picking up Taco and petting the cat as he watched me spoon dinner into serving bowls. "Well, I'm happy to help. Anything other than the work I brought home with me tonight."

I handed him a bowl to carry in to the dining room and took the other. "You work too much. I work too much. We need to not work and do something with the kids this weekend."

"Come join us Saturday for Madison's cross country meet. We can all go out for pizza afterward, if you don't mind cramming into the car with a bunch of sweaty teenagers."

"I'd love that."

I *would* love that. Like a family. I'd be sharing this slice of their lives, and hopefully over the next year or two, I'd be able to share even more. We all sat at the table, Henry still teasing Madison about her driving. I loved having us all here together. I loved my little adopted family.

"What is this?" Madison asked as she peered into one of the bowls. "Is this rice?"

"Quinoa," I told her. "Some people use it in place of rice. I thought I'd try something different."

The girl shrugged and scooped it onto her plate, layering the chicken stir fry on top. "Sounds good to me. I'm starved."

"Real men don't eat quinoas," Henry lamented, poking a fork at his dinner.

"Real men politely eat what they're served and tell their host or hostess it was an amazing meal," Judge Beck rebuked. "Real men are unafraid to try something new. Real men know that a funny-sounding food might be really good."

Henry glanced up at me with an apologetic smile. "Sorry, Miss Kay. I didn't mean to insult your cooking or anything. Thanks for making dinner."

"If you don't like it, you can always get a sandwich," I told him.

"No, I'm gonna eat it." The boy took a big breath and scooped some onto his fork. "Real men are brave. Real men eat the weird-looking rice stuff with the funny name and manage to keep it down and not go get a sandwich. Real man here, working up the nerve to take a bite of this stuff."

I laughed. "Real men know that a home-cooked meal is more than just food. There's a love in those grains that satisfies the heart just as much as the belly."

"Real women who just spent two hours at cross-country

practice don't really care what's on the plate because they're starving." Madison crammed a huge bite into her mouth. "It's good. Eat it, you wimp."

"Don't talk with your mouth full," her father told her. "And Henry, if that food isn't in your mouth in two seconds, you're grounded from your phone for the night."

The boy shoved the forkful into his mouth, wrinkling his nose as he chewed and swallowed. "Dinner is wonderful, Miss Kay. Thank you so much."

"Liar," I teased. "Let me get you a sandwich."

"No, you most certainly will not get him a sandwich," Judge Beck told me. "He's going to eat what's on his plate, and then when he's done with that, he can make his own sandwich if he wants."

I gave Henry a sympathetic glance. "There's pumpkin bars for when we're done. And I promise no more quinoa in the future."

The lure of pumpkin bars had both kids eating their dinner in record time. Judge Beck had them carry the dishes into the kitchen, and I gave them each two pumpkin bars to eat while they worked on their homework.

While they worked, Judge Beck and I did the dishes while I told him all about Melvin Elmer.

"He needs a lawyer," the judge insisted, scooping the leftover stir fry into a plastic container. "A lawyer will get a temporary stay on the eviction of a week or so, and that will give him enough time to pull together proof that the man never took out that mortgage, and that the lender had no legal right to a lien on the house, and thus no basis for foreclosure. Once his lawyer shows the court that there's an issue involving the property title, the eviction will remain on hold. We're not monsters, Kay. None of us wants to kick a dying ninety-year-old man onto the street. We need to uphold what appears to be a legitimate claim to a title, but give us an excuse, and we'll put a hold on it."

"Mr. Elmer says that he went to a lawyer," I said as I rinsed the dishes. "He can't afford the guy. And he doesn't want to spend the last six months of his life dealing with ongoing litigation. Why is Spencer Thompson such a jerk? Why? If he'd just give the man six months, he could have the house after Mr. Elmer dies. Six darned months, and he wouldn't need to have to sue the mortgage company to get his investment back or deal with any losses."

"Some people are heartless," the judge agreed.

"What can he do outside of hiring a lawyer?" I asked. "There has to be some other way he can remain in his home until he dies."

"There aren't many other choices, Kay. Mr. Elmer can ask to have the eviction postponed himself by coming into the courthouse and filing the paperwork. That's not unusual. People get a few extra days or weeks due to hardship, or bad weather. To get anything longer, though, we'd need to see a pending court case. We'd need to have an indication that the foreclosure, and Brockhurst Properties' claim on the title, might not be legitimate. We can't just do that based on his word. We need to see that there's an ongoing legal proceeding to put all this on hold more than a week or so."

He was right, but it didn't make me feel any better. I put my head in my hands and leaned against the sink, my eyes stinging with tears.

A hand rubbed my back, warm and firm. "Have Mr. Elmer talk to social services about possibly finding a pro-bono lawyer. Or maybe that non-profit place can help. That Humble House place you were talking about."

I lifted my head to find Judge Beck behind me, his hand on my shoulder, his face full of concern. "I left a message for Tracey Abramson, but they do reverse mortgages and equity payouts. They can't do that for a man who can't prove he owns the home anymore."

He sighed, giving my shoulder a quick squeeze. "It doesn't sound like Mr. Elmer has anyone to take care of him or help him in his last months, or that he has money for a home health aide. Maybe fighting this isn't the best use of his remaining six months. He could stay with friends, or in a small apartment, then when things get bad, move into a hospice facility."

"He wants to die at home. And I completely understand what that feels like," I choked out.

"Because Eli wanted to die here?" he asked, his voice gentle.

"I never seriously thought of putting Eli in a home," I told him. "No matter how hard it got. Ten years he lived after his accident. I wouldn't have wanted him to be in a nursing home for ten years."

"But Mr. Elmer only has six months. And you know people who are happy in facilities that provide nursing care. Matt's father is happy, isn't he?"

"Matt's father always asks when he's going home," I countered. "Half the time he thinks his wife is still alive and waiting for him. The other half he thinks Matt is going to take care of him. I don't fault Matt one bit for having his father at Tranquil Meadows. Only he can decide where his father will be safe and provided with the care he needs, but in spite of that, the man would rather be in his own home."

"Kay, not everyone can afford home health care, or a live-in nurse. In an ideal situation, Brockhurst Properties would delay the eviction, but legally they don't have to."

"It's not just that," I told him. "I want this to be made right. I don't want a mortgage company or Spencer Thompson to profit from a case of identity theft. It's not right."

"Giving out a hundred-thousand-dollar loan and only getting fifty thousand at the foreclosure sale isn't my idea of profiting, but I understand what you mean. You want justice served. I do too. It's kind of my job, you know."

I gave him a wobbly smile. "I know. I'm sorry. I didn't mean to dump all this on you. I'm just so frustrated, and I feel a bit helpless to remedy the situation."

"Sometimes all you can do is deliver partial justice. Do that. Do what you can within the scope of your job and abilities, then let it go. You can't always be King Solomon. Sometimes you have to be satisfied with a fine for jaywalking and let someone further down the line work on dividing the baby."

I took a deep breath. "Thanks. You're right. Partial justice. I'll do what I can and hope that someone else can do what I can't."

Originally, this case had been about finding hidden assets for a divorce hearing, but now I wanted to find a way to let Mr. Elmer stay in his home for as long as he could.

And make sure Spencer Thompson's wife knew what her husband had been up to over the last five years of their marriage.

CHAPTER 10

*M*y heart wasn't into yoga the next morning. All I could think about was poor Mr. Elmer and how I could possibly help him. Daisy and I cut our exercise short, and I'd showered and headed out, taking the remaining pumpkin bars and some apricot scones with me as potential bribes. I got the feeling I'd need them.

Marissa Thompson was actually waiting for me at the coffee shop this morning, looking forlorn as she sat alone at a table with her cup in hand. I detailed what I'd found out so far—about her husband's partnership in an LLC with Tracey Abramson, as well as his suspected ownership of Brockhurst Properties.

"But where is the money?" she demanded, her hand so tight on the coffee cup that she was nearly crushing it. "If he had this other company, he certainly wasn't getting any of his pay deposited into our joint account. Five years? That must add up to hundreds of thousands of dollars in income."

I didn't blame her one bit for being angry. I would be too if I'd been in her shoes. "It should be easy for your lawyer to gain access to that deposit information once you file for divorce," I assured her. "And I'm sure there's income in Brockhurst Properties as well. They've bought at least one home at a foreclosure sale, so there has to be a checking account somewhere."

"None of this was on our taxes," she said between clenched teeth. "None of it. And where did he get the money for this partnership with this Tracey woman? Are they sleeping together? Maybe he's kept all the money in her name so I won't be able to get any of it."

I eyed her in alarm, worried that there was about to be a scene in the coffee shop, complete with screaming and a latte hurled across the room. "Tracey Abramson isn't a woman. He's a man. My age or older from what I can see. He's married, and I don't get the impression he had anything other than a business partnership with your husband. In fact, it sounds like things are not good between the two of them. Mr. Abramson has been trying to dissolve the LLC for the last few years."

I thought that would calm her down, but if anything, she seemed to become even more angry.

"There's no woman. None. He's just hiding all this money from me, running these other businesses on the side and not letting me know. That bastard. That rat bastard. How could he do this to me? How?"

I'd thought of telling her about Melvin Elmer, perhaps enlisting her help in getting her husband to hold off on the eviction, but I now realized that wasn't a good idea. Marissa Thompson didn't look like she was in the mood to be asking her soon-to-be ex-husband for favors, and I was worried that letting her know Spencer was kicking a terminally ill old man out of his home would just be throwing gasoline on the fire.

"You have every right to be angry, Mrs. Thompson," I assured her. "I'll continue to find out what I can about these two businesses and any income your husband may have earned from them, but I think you really need to share this information with your lawyer. He can advise you on how to proceed and the best timing for things going forward."

"How much?" She snapped. "How much do you think he has between these two businesses?"

"I can look into the net worth of the LLC, but that won't tell me the details of the partnership arrangement and how much of that is your husband's. I'll continue to research, but you probably should speak with your lawyer about the next steps."

"The next steps I take are going to be over my husband's dead body." She stood and snatched her purse off the back of her chair. "I thought maybe there were some gambling winnings, or a little side investment, but this? The man might have half a million stashed somewhere. Two businesses, and he never told me about either of them?"

"Please talk to your lawyer before you do anything rash, Mrs. Thompson," I pleaded with her. Where was J.T. when I needed him? He would have known how to calm this woman down.

"Too late," she snapped. Then she spun around on her heels and stormed through the door. I heard her car squeal out of the lot as I took a few calming breaths and gathered up my own things, hoping that Mrs. Thompson went home, broke a few dishes, then called her lawyer as I advised. Either way, I needed to let J.T. know what was going on. I'd been so busy yesterday and this morning that I hadn't even seen him, and other than a quick update yesterday after I'd met with Tracey Abramson, I hadn't spoken with him. He didn't know about Brockhurst Properties, or Melvin Elmer.

Tracey Abramson returned my call on my way into the office. It seems Melvin Elmer had reached out to them the day he'd gotten the eviction notice, but they'd told the man they were unable to help him, and that he should contact a lawyer.

"He doesn't have the money for a lawyer," I said, narrowly avoiding a parked car in my distracted state. "He's elderly and terminally ill. Someone stole his identity and now he's lost his house due to fraud. He needs help."

"He needs a lawyer," Tracey said firmly, reminding me very much of Judge Beck at the moment. "We provide reverse mortgage services and other similar services. I can't grant a program to someone when their home title is in question. The whole thing is a mess and this isn't something our foundation deals with. He needs a lawyer."

Once in the office, I worked on some of the Creditcorp skip traces, and organized my data on the Thompson case, the whole time watching the phone and waiting for J.T. to arrive. I nearly tackled him when he walked through the door.

"Oh, thank God you're here! Spencer Thompson has another business and he's evicting a dying ninety-year-old man who lost his house because of identity theft and when I spoke to Mrs. Thompson this morning to brief her on the case, she completely lost it and stormed out of the coffee shop in anger. She's furious her husband was doing all this behind her back. I told her to talk to her lawyer, but she's so angry. Was there something else I should have done? What should I have done?"

"Calm down, Kay." J.T. put a hand on my shoulder and pressed me gently back into my chair. "Clients are going to get upset in this business, especially with these divorce cases. I'm sure you did fine. She'll calm down, go talk to her lawyer, then call us with further instructions. In the meantime, type it all up and tally your hours, and we'll be prepared to send her our findings and the invoice if she's ready to turn it over to her lawyer."

I took a deep breath. "He's listed as a partner on the LLC and Tracey Abramson confirmed it, so all Mrs. Thompson needs to do is have her lawyer contact them for the details of the business arrangement as well as what was paid out to her husband over the years, but this other business, this Brockhurst Properties... All I have is a tip that Spencer Thompson is connected, a property tax payment that links him and the company, and the word of a ninety-year-old man that says Thompson is involved. I hate to turn that over to Mrs. Thompson's lawyer until I'm sure."

Once again, J.T. motioned for me to breathe. "You said in your text that there was an eviction filing? I called for the transcript copies. If Spencer Thompson is involved, he might be listed on those. If not, then if Mrs. Thompson wants, we'll do more digging."

"Oh, and do you know any lawyers who might be willing to take a pro-bono case on identity theft of the elderly? Or perhaps a lawyer who might be willing to do a payment plan?"

Find a lawyer. Get the eviction transcripts. Look at the Deed of Trust and Promissory note for the fraudulent mortgage, plus anything else Violet had managed to turn up. It wasn't just about helping our client at this point. I was determined to find anything I could that might help Melvin Elmer and keep him in his house.

J.T. grabbed a chair and wheeled it over, sitting down next to me. Drat. This wasn't a good sign.

"Kay, you're taking on too much here. We have a paying client. Find out what you can on Brockhurst Properties for Mrs. Thompson and type up the findings and the invoice. I know you want to help this man, but you can't do everything. You can't help everyone."

"But it's related," I countered. "It appears that Spencer Thompson owns the company that bought his house at auction. If I can find some information on how he paid for these things, I might be able to track down the bank accounts for Mrs. Thompson."

J.T. shot me a knowing glance. "Chasing down a Deed of Trust and Promissory note that Thompson had nothing to do with isn't helping Mrs. Thompson's case. I understand where you might want to help this man, Kay, but business needs to come first. You're running yourself ragged with all this."

"He's being evicted on Monday," I insisted. "If I don't hurry, it will be too late and Thompson will be in possession of the home. By the time this gets resolved, if it ever does get resolved, the house will be sold."

"Then Mr. Elmer will get the proceeds," J.T. reminded me. "He'll get all the profits from the house sale, plus a settlement from the mortgage company."

"If he wins. And even if he does win and get money, that's not what he wants. He's dying, J.T. He wants to live out the last of his days in his home. By the time this court case is resolved, he'll be dead. All I want is to get enough evidence to convince an investigative reporter to take it on, or to convince a sympathetic lawyer to take it on, or to convince the sheriff's office to stay the eviction."

J.T. sighed and rubbed a hand over his face. "Okay, but our cases can't miss deadlines because of this. Call Miles. He's probably assisted at more evictions than I have fingers and toes. He'll tell you what forms Mr. Elmer should fill out to get a temporary stay, especially if you've got something good in that basket on your desk. You're going to the courthouse anyway. Have him meet you."

It was a great idea. I stood and gave J.T. a hug, which he returned awkwardly, then grabbed my purse and basket and headed out, calling Miles as I drove.

The first thing I did was pick up was the transcripts,

noting that the clerk J.T. had called also helpfully included copies of the forms to begin the process as well as those requesting the sheriff's office to serve the notices. The paperwork listed Brockhurst Properties as the plaintiff along with an address and phone number, and a signature by Spencer Thompson. As soon as I got back to the office, I'd do a search on the address to see what I could find. At the very least, Marissa Thompson would have proof that her husband was operating another side business and be able to have her lawyer demand those financials as well as the ones from Humble Properties, LLC.

Heading downstairs, I met Violet, who had the mortgage paperwork copies ready for me. The pair of us looked over them on a bench outside in the hallway.

"Everything looks in order," she told me.

"Except that it's not." I pulled the eviction transcripts from my bag, hoping to compare the signatures, only to realize that Melvin Elmer had never signed either set of documents. Violet looked over my shoulder at the eviction paperwork and pointed to the sheet authorizing the sheriff's office to act as process servers for the eviction notices.

"You know, I can probably find a copy of the check he used to pay for the process service. He might have screwed up and paid the county taxes with his personal account, but I'll bet he used a business account for this one."

She was right. And if there had been a payment to the sheriff's office in those bank statements, eagle-eyed Violet would have found it.

"That would be incredible!" I exclaimed. "Do you think you could get it for me by the end of the day?"

If I could get Mrs. Thompson an actual bank account, we'd have a happy client. Especially if I could nose into the account using the list of passwords she'd provided and verify the amount of money in there. People tended to reuse the same passwords for multiple accounts. There was a good chance that Spencer Thompson had done the same.

I thanked Violet again for her help, gave her a scone, then headed upstairs to meet Miles, briefcase on one arm and basket of baked goods on the other. Miles was a welcome sight, insisting that he'd be happy to help me, even if I hadn't brought pumpkin bars and scones. He provided me with some paperwork that would give Melvin Elmer an extra two weeks as a hardship stay, then like everyone else I'd spoken with in the last twenty-four hours, insisted that the best way to ensure Mr. Elmer spent his remaining days in his home would be for him to hire a lawyer.

"I really don't want to put an elderly man out on the street," Miles told me between bites of pumpkin bar. "But we can't really do more than a two-week extension without there being something in process questioning the validity of the property title. And that's not something a civilian can really do themselves. He needs a lawyer."

"He can't afford one," I told him, repeating the same excuse I'd given over and over again.

"Blow it up on social media. Get the talking heads on the news involved. There's an ambulance chaser out there who will be willing to make a name for themselves on something like this. Plus, those litigation attorneys are used to getting paid on settlement. It's how their whole business works. Ask Judge Beck to tell you the name of one he hates seeing in court the most. They're sharks and they're masters at spinning public opinion. Get one of them involved and Brockhurst Properties will voluntarily hold off on the eviction to keep a hundred-thousand one-star Yelp reviews from flooding his business."

I didn't think Spencer Thompson cared much about Yelp reviews as a property flipper, but Miles did have a point. A divorce was going to be bad enough without a highly public case making him seem like a horrible villain at the same time.

Melvin Elmer *did* need a lawyer. And I was going to help him find one. First, I'd wrap up this Thompson case and ensure Mr. Elmer had these papers filed to grant him the eviction stay. Then I'd get as much information out in public about the injustice of an elderly, terminally ill victim of identity theft losing his house. Then I'd find the nastiest bulldog of an attorney I could find to take his case.

And hopefully, Mr. Elmer would be able to see those bulbs bloom next spring.

CHAPTER 11

*M*iles helped me fill out the petition to delay the eviction, and I ran by Mr. Elmer's house hoping to get his signature on the papers and file them on my way back from my appointment at Fullbright and Mason. No one answered the door, so I tucked it all inside an envelope and wrote a quick explanation on the front before I wedged it in the screen door, praying as I left that Mr. Elmer actually opened that envelope and didn't just pitch it thinking it was more junk mail.

I had a secondary motive in wanting to run the signed paperwork by the courthouse myself. Yes, I wanted to help this man as much as I could, but there was that pragmatic side of me that had been a journalist whispering a mantra into my brain. Check and double check—sources, information, and everything. It was too easy when writing a story or investigating a case to get excited and charge ahead on a false lead. I didn't want to make J.T.'s company look bad or make myself look like an idiot. So I wanted to check Melvin Elmer's signature against those on the Deed of Trust and Promissory note. I believed Mr. Elmer, but I wasn't naive enough to believe that I was incapable of being fooled. Time was running out, but if I was going to splash this story all over social media and get the television involved, I wanted to make sure there really was an identity theft, and not just a man wanting sympathy for his poor financial decisions.

I pulled into the parking lot at Fullbright and Mason with a scant ten minutes before my appointment and nearly sprinted through the front doors, tapping my foot impatiently as I waited for the elevator. It was a short ride. Locust Point didn't have any buildings over three stories, but Milford had several that reached to what was for us skyscraper status at six floors. Thankfully the offices of Fullbright and Mason were on the third.

The elevator opened to a sea of glass with shining chrome handles on the double doors and silver etching above. They were the only office on this floor according to the directory, and anyone exiting the elevator had a clear view right in to the receptionist desk and what appeared to be two sets of conference rooms flanking it to the back. I heaved one of the huge glass doors open, signed my name in the guest log, and returned the receptionist's bright smile and greeting. Within a few minutes, a young well-dressed man who was not Spencer Thompson came and escorted me back.

We passed through a maze of desks, all with people chatting on the phones or typing into computers. The offices along the outer wall were clearly reserved for the executives. It made me wonder how Spencer felt working among the masses in a cubicle. From what I'd gathered, he seemed like the mover and shaker type. I was sure in a lesser firm he would have probably warranted an office with a window. There was always a trade-off to be had in working for a big-name blue-chip company, and that's exactly what Fullbright and Mason was. Headquarters and major offices in all the huge metropolises, and these smaller but still ostentatious satellite offices in smaller cities. Taking up the entire third floor in this not-so-huge building wasn't quite as impressive as it sounded, and I quickly figured there were probably ten people warranting the offices and maybe two dozen analysts and advisors out in the mosh pit.

The well-dressed young man led me to a large cubicle, separated from the others with tall dividers. A U-shaped desk took up most of the space, with a computer off to the side and folders neatly stacked and color coordinated in the back. As Spencer Thompson rose to greet me and shake my hand, I noticed the sparsity of personal items in his office space. There was a picture of him and his wife that appeared to be from early, happier days in their marriage. It looked professional, with the sort of pose and composition and emotion of the pictures that came with the frame. Other than that, the only item that hinted at the occupant's personality was a huge white mug of coffee with a gold dollar sign emblazoned on it. It was on one of those hot-plate thingies that kept your giant mug of coffee hot all day while you sipped from it.

The mug was Spencer Thompson. The picture I took to be a carefully selected prop. And I could tell from the guarded expression on Mr. Thompson's face that he'd done some research in preparation for our appointment. He had the look of someone who felt this meeting was going to be a complete waste of his time but didn't want to offend me in case I'd just inherited a windfall from an ancient aunt or had a savings account not evident from my lifestyle or public records or credit reports.

He was quickly going to learn his earlier assumption was correct.

"So, Mrs. Carrera. I'm so sorry to have learned of your recent loss. My condolences. Your husband was a notable surgeon."

And I was sure he'd gotten that from a quick Google search.

"Yes, Mr. Thompson. I'm hoping you can help me. I'm trying to find out what options are available to me as far as planning my retirement and my future estate. I'm hoping to lay the groundwork for a retirement in the next five years."

"I see." From the befuddled look in his eyes, he didn't see, but was still holding out hope for my being an eccentric with hidden assets. "Let's start with your current investments and savings."

"I'm afraid I don't have any current investments," I confessed.

"That's okay," he said with an uncertain smile. "I meet with lots of people your age who were reluctant to trust their money in the stock market. I'm assuming you stuck with CDs or property?"

I shook my head.

"Money under the mattress?"

I had to give it to the guy, that was pretty funny. "No. I only have five hundred in savings. I've been building it up over the last six months. My husband's disability and medical needs depleted our retirement accounts and savings."

His face fell. "Was there an insurance settlement? From what I understand, there was an accident...?"

I nodded. "Yes, but the initial medical costs were very high, and at the time I'd assumed he'd make a recovery, so I settled for a lump sum to pay the immediate bills and for his physical and cognitive therapy."

"So there's nothing left of that settlement?"

"No. It was gone within two years and I needed to cash out the 401k." People had no idea how high out-of-pocket medical costs could go, especially when you were desperate. I happily spent every last dime on whatever treatment gave me even a tiny chance of improvement in Eli's physical or mental function. And as far as I'd been concerned, none of it had been money wasted. Yes, we'd pretty much gone broke. Yes, he'd had many days of deep despair and frustration, as had I. No, nothing had been a miracle cure to get him anywhere close to who he'd been before the accident. But that money, both the settlement and the retirement savings, had primarily been built from his income and from the settlement from the accident that took so much from him. I couldn't deny him a cent of that money if it offered even a slim chance at improvement, no matter if it meant I had to be his sole caretaker, to mortgage our home to the hilt, to sacrifice any chance I had at ease in retirement.

Was that why Eli's ghost still lingered? Did he carry guilt over how much I'd given as I carried over how I should have done more? We'd built our nest egg for a joint retirement, both of us dreaming of travel and a house at the beach, of not worrying about the costs of home repairs or new cars, of being stress free in our elderly years. He'd always insisted it was our money, not his, that a married couple was a partnership, a unit, of two becoming one. Did his spirit mourn that he'd sucked up every bit of that money, leaving me with nothing?

Oh, Eli. You would have done the same for me had our positions been reversed. I regret only that I couldn't do more, that sometimes I didn't have the patience I should have.

"Well, let's look at your house, then." Mr. Thompson pulled a file from the stack behind him. "Wow. That's a gorgeous Victorian, Mrs. Carrera. It looks to be well maintained as well. Perhaps you can do an equity loan at a low interest rate and use that to base an investment strategy on."

"I already have two mortgages on the house," I told him. "If I sold it right now, I might clear enough to pay off those plus the closing costs. There's really no equity in my home at the moment."

He sat down the folder with a slap, a muscle twitching in his jaw. "I really don't know how I can help you then, Mrs. Carrera. What exactly are you looking to gain from this meeting?"

It had been a Hail Mary shot to get a feel for Spencer Thompson in my quest to track down any of his hidden assets, but I had a good handle on that. Right now, my goal had changed, and there was something very different I wanted from him.

But not quite yet. The optimist in me was still looking for something good about this man. Something that I might appeal to on behalf of Melvin Elmer.

"I've taken in a roommate to pay the mortgage, and I'm able to put a few hundred away each month in savings. I got a raise this month. I'm hoping you can give me a strategy to follow so that I can retire in the next five years."

He glared at me, his hands coming down with a thump on his desk. "I'm sorry, Mrs. Carrera, but you'll never be able to retire. You squandered whatever income your husband had so skillfully accumulated during his lifetime, and you're now poor. The minute your house needs a new roof, that few hundred a month in savings is going to go to zero. You're living paycheck to paycheck. You'll have to continue working for the rest of your life. And the moment you can't find a roommate or can't afford to maintain this huge home of yours, you'll need to sell it and go live in a cardboard box somewhere. This is what happens when women blow all the money their husbands save."

I felt my blood pressure rise, a white-hot anger course through me. This...this *bastard*. How dare he assume that I'd frittered away all of Eli's—all of *our*—savings on purses and facials. The man was a pig. But somehow, I managed to rein in my fury and swallow it down so I could ask for the one thing I really wanted out of this meeting—a six-month stay on Mr. Elmer's eviction.

"I thought you helped the elderly, Mr. Thompson. I thought that was your mission here at Fullbright and Mason, as well as your personal mission judging by your bio on the company website."

He fixed me with a hard stare. "I help those who help themselves, Mrs. Carrera. I'm not a charity for people who have made poor choices in their lives. And neither is Fullbright and Mason. We can't help you. I can't help you." He stood and extended his hand. "Best of luck to you. Have a nice day."

I remained seated. "There's someone else you can help, someone who hasn't made poor choices in his life. He doesn't have much in the way of savings, but he owns his home free and clear."

Mr. Thompson hesitated. "Tell him to come see me. He could do a reverse mortgage, and I'd be happy to help him invest that money."

"He can't. Someone stole his identity and took out a mortgage in his name. He didn't know about it and they foreclosed on the house. He's being evicted."

The man's face hardened. "Then he needs a lawyer, not a financial advisor. Good day, Mrs. Carrera."

"He's dying, Mr. Thompson. All he wants is six months, to stay in the house until he dies. Then you can have it. Six months is all you have to wait, and that beats all the bad publicity you're going to get when this blows up. Kicking a terminally ill elderly man out of his home after he'd lost it due to identity theft? Everyone is going to know your name and know Brockhurst Properties preys on vulnerable people. How do you think Fullbright and Mason would feel about having you as one of their investment counselors once this is on the nightly news? Just six months is all he wants."

"Get out now!" Spencer Thompson shouted, pointing toward the exit of his cubicle. A few passersby stopped to gawk at the two of us.

"Six months," I pleaded. "Six months and no one needs to know and you'll get to sell the house at a profit."

Well, no one needed to know but his soon-to-be ex-wife, anyway.

"Out before I call the police!" His face was red and puffy, bits of spittle flying as he shouted. It wasn't a good look.

And I had my answer.

"Fine. I'm leaving." I got to my feet. "But you'll regret this decision, Mr. Thompson. You're going to regret it."

I wasn't sure what he screamed at me as I hurried through the hallways and out of the offices of Fullbright and Mason, but I was determined Spencer Thompson was going to go down. His wife was going to take him for every cent he had, and if I had to empty my savings and pay for a lawyer, Mr. Elmer was going to get his house back.

Yes, Spencer Thompson would rue the day he'd said "no" to me.

CHAPTER 12

$\mathcal{M}$elvin Elmer was home when I stopped by on my way back to the office, and thankfully he hadn't just pitched the envelope I'd left for him in the trash.

"You really think this is going to work?" he asked as he peered at the paper.

"It will only give you a few weeks, but the deputy I spoke to seems to think he can make it happen. It will give you time to get a lawyer on this."

He shook his head. "I don't want to bother with lawyers and all that. I'm dying, Mrs. Carrera. I just want to enjoy my last months in my home."

"I know that but hiring a lawyer will let you do just that," I urged. "Scams against the elderly garner huge publicity. There's someone that will take this on for payment after it settles. We just need the time to find that lawyer. And once you do, he'll handle it all and you can just enjoy your remaining time here in your own home."

"I don't have any children. No nieces or nephews. Nobody to inherit this house. Don't get me wrong, Mrs. Carrera. I love this home of mine, and I love every plant out in my garden. I want it all to go to someone who loves it, but that someone doesn't have to be a distant relative. The lawyer can have it when I die. I'd have given it to that nasty Spencer Thompson man if he'd let me stay here until I died. Given it to him." He sighed and signed the paperwork, handing it back to me. "Anyone else would have seen the wisdom in that, but not that spawn of the devil."

"That's why we're going to have to play hardball." I tucked the paperwork in my bag. "Miles is going to get you two more weeks. Once I get this story on the local news and all over social media, we'll get you a lawyer."

He nodded but seemed distracted.

"Is everything okay, Mr. Elmer? Is there something I can pick up for you or do for you while I'm here?" Old habits die hard. I'd spent the last ten years being a caretaker for my husband, and now I wanted to do all I could for this man in his final days.

He gave me a tired smile. "I think I'm good. Just gonna go lay down for a bit. Thank you for all you've done for me. I'm thinking it's all gonna be okay."

"It will be," I told him as I headed out the door. "It will be. I feel it in my bones."

As I drove toward the courthouse, I began to worry about the repercussion of my little confrontation at Fullbright and Mason. Had Spencer Thompson called the police? Registered some kind of complaint? Perhaps he'd taken my parting words as a threat and was right now filing for a restraining order.

Oh, no. Could I lose my job over this? Would our case be compromised? I shouldn't have lost my temper like that. I should have just left. He'd clearly shown himself to be a heartless jerk from the way he'd talked to Mr. Elmer. I hardly needed to have an argument with him in the middle of his office to prove that.

What the heck was going on with me? I never normally would have done something like that. No, who was I kidding? Before Eli's accident, I'd been impulsive and prone to taking risks. I'd do anything when on a lead, and I'd been fearless when confronting anyone from politicians to trash collectors if I needed to get a story. Maybe I was just coming back into my own after a long hibernation of worry and concern while taking care of Eli. Maybe this was me.

And maybe me was gonna get me fired if I didn't start thinking before I had an argument with a client's soon-to-be-ex in his office. I wasn't a journalist any longer; I was a private investigator. And I needed to act like one.

I dropped the papers off at the courthouse, giving the signatures a quick compare before I did. Melvin Elmer's swirly mark on the request to stay eviction was nothing like the bold, sharp scribble on the loan paperwork. Nothing. I guess identity thievery only went so far, and any attempt at forgery was more effort than it was worth.

On my way out, I was accosted by Violet, running down the hall with a set of papers in her hand. She shoved them into my hands then stood back, beaming.

I unfolded them and saw a copy of a check. It was from Brockhurst Properties and was signed by Spencer Thompson. It was made out to the sheriff's office, with a note in the memo section that this was for an eviction service.

I had it. A routing number. An account number. I still regretted that I'd made a scene at his office, but now I had definitive proof of a business and banking account his wife had not known of. We'd earned our fees, and hopefully I hadn't screwed things up to an unforgivable level.

CHAPTER 13

"*B*ut wait, there's more!" I exclaimed to J.T. as I walked through the office door. "I've actually got an account number now, and..." My voice trailed off as I saw J.T. standing next to a man I recognized—Detective Desmond Keeler from the Milford Police Department. I'd met him when he was investigating Luanne Trainor's murder and it hadn't been a pleasant experience—neither the murder nor meeting Detective Keeler.

I doubted he was there reconsidering a starring role in one of J.T.'s YouTube videos. Was he here to elicit our help on one of his cases?

"Kay," my boss began, "Detective Keeler is here to ask you a few questions about your visit to Fullbright and Mason earlier today."

My heart sank clear into my shoes. That rat Thompson had called the police on me, and they must have taken it seriously if they'd sent a detective to scold me.

Wait. An officer would have come to question me, not a detective. I knew that much about police affairs. And although Milford was small enough that the detectives on their city police force weren't specialized, my only experience with Keeler was in homicide.

"Ask away." I gestured to a chair and sat in the one in front of my desk, putting my bags to the side.

The detective sat, pulling out a little notepad and a pen. "So, you had an appointment with Spencer Thompson at one o'clock. What was the nature of your meeting?"

"Investment advice. He specializes in estate and retirement planning." I wasn't going to give this jerk anything more than the bare minimum, and I certainly wasn't going to violate client confidentiality, either. Slap me on the wrist. I'll never do it again. Lost my temper. Blah, blah.

"So, you have a significant estate to plan?" His eyebrows lifted. "Investments and savings you need to have managed by a financial advisor?"

Did everyone in Milford know I was poor? I'd expected this in Locust Point, but how had the rumors of my poverty spread to the neighboring city?

"No, but I felt he might be able to give me some advice on going forward. What my best options would be in trying to save for my golden years."

"I take it his answers were not satisfactory as..." he flipped back a few pages in his notebook, "coworkers say the pair of you were shouting at each other and Mr. Thompson repeatedly told you to leave."

"He was very insulting. I lost my temper and we exchanged words." I sent an apologetic glance J.T.'s way. "I left immediately after that and I don't intend on returning. There's no need to bar me from the place or anything."

"Witnesses say that you told him 'You're going to regret this'?"

I looked again at a scowling J.T. and began to be nervous about my continued employment. I didn't want Detective Keeler to know that I was there pleading for Spencer

Thompson to hold off evicting someone, nor that the man's wife was about to file for divorce, so I had to look like the idiot yelling at a man over his inability to turn my five-hundred-dollar savings account into a retirement income stream.

"I did say that, but I think you and I both know that I didn't mean it as a physical threat. I'm a sixty-year-old woman, Detective Keeler. Spencer Thompson outweighs me by fifty to seventy pounds. I'm hardly going to accost him in the parking lot."

He leaned back in his chair. "So you meant the threat to be what, exactly? That you were going to win big on lottery scratch-offs and he'd rue the day he'd turned down handling your portfolio?"

I grimaced. "Something like that. He was rude and insulting, but I was not making a threat upon his person."

The detective made a little note in his book. "And when you left his office, where exactly did you go?"

This was getting ridiculous. I knew Detective Keeler didn't like me, but this interrogation was way out of place for a simple complaint.

"I had to pick up some signed documents, then I went to the courthouse. I was at the courthouse by quarter after two. There are several people there that can vouch for my presence. Why? Did someone try to assault Spencer Thompson outside his office? Look at me, Detective Keeler. I'm pretty fit for a woman my age, but I'm not exactly the sort of person who would physically attack a man in a parking lot in the middle of the day."

"Not attack, kill." He slid the notepad back into this jacket pocket and clicked the pen. "Spencer Thompson is dead, Mrs. Carrera."

I shot another glance at J.T., who was clearly just as shocked as I was. "Dead? How...who..."

"The 'who' is what I'm trying to determine. The how is poison. Specifically poison in his coffee."

Coffee. I eyed the half-empty cup on my own desk and shuddered, remembering Spencer's dollar-sign festooned mug on the warmer.

My mind whirled with thoughts. I'd spoken with his wife this morning and she'd been furious, but poison was a far cry from grabbing a knife off the counter in the heat of an argument. Poison took thought and planning, and while I knew in my gut that Marissa Thompson was capable of such a thing, I couldn't see her having the motive. Unless she wanted all of Spencer's money and not just half of it.

The wife might have somewhat of a motive, but I clearly didn't.

"Poison. What kind of poison?" I demanded.

Detective Keeler watched me carefully as he spoke. "We're not sure yet. It was powerful and fast-acting. A coworker said they were bringing him a file when he took a big gulp from his mug and promptly spit it out across the desk. He was screaming and clawing at his mouth and throat and began to cough and vomit blood. She immediately called for an ambulance, but he was dead before it arrived."

Holy cow. I stared openmouthed at the detective, horrified by his narrative and a bit surprised that he'd revealed such details to me when in my experience, he'd always been stingy about keeping information close to his vest.

I cleared my throat and organized my thoughts for a moment. "No one else in the office was affected?"

He shook his head. "We pulled all the coffee pots as well as the packets of grounds to test, just in case. With thirty-five people working there today and no one else showing symptoms, we believe Spencer Thompson was the sole target."

Not the office in general then, which meant either a client was angry at Spencer, or his wife had decided to take all their assets instead of half, or there was a disgruntled business partner, lover, or golf buddy, or anyone who'd slipped something into the man's cup.

"Well, it obviously wasn't me. Spencer Thompson didn't leave his cubicle during our meeting. I wouldn't have had the opportunity to slip something into his cup unobserved. And I had no reason to want him dead. It's not like I walk around with a box of rat poison in my purse just in case some investment counselor insults me."

"You could have returned afterward," Detective Keeler reminded me.

"After I made that huge scene?" I scoffed. "I wouldn't have gotten past the receptionist desk. It wasn't me. And you know it wasn't me or I would be down at the police station right now."

He nodded, a hint of a smile curling up the edge of his mouth. "He saw no other appointments after you. He died within ten minutes of you leaving. A bit of a coincidence, don't you think?"

"Yes, I do think." And I was thinking something else as well. "Spencer Thompson didn't touch his coffee the whole time I was there. He had it on one of those warmer things. It could have been poisoned before I got there."

His eyebrows lifted again. "Who pours a cup of coffee and leaves it sit for an hour untouched?"

I waved at my own half-empty mug. "Someone busy, that's who. And he had a warmer under it, so he wouldn't dump it out and get some fresh from down the hall. Maybe not hours and hours, but definitely check an hour or so before I got there. Or maybe his coworkers. One of them might have slipped something in his mug after I left. That woman delivering the files, maybe."

"So, who do you think might have wanted Spencer

Thompson dead?" he asked, still clicking his pen and eyeing me intently.

Ah. Clearly my acting skills were worse than I'd thought. He hadn't believed my sole reason for visiting Mr. Thompson was for personal investment advice. Before I could speak up, J.T. did.

"As much as we want to assist the police, especially in something as serious as a murder investigation, we do have client confidentiality to consider," my boss said.

"I'm not asking for client lists or details." Detective Keeler turned his eagle-eye gaze toward J.T "I just want to know that if either of you has reason to suspect someone you know of murdering Spencer Thompson, or have information material to the case, you'll contact me. To withhold that information would be...problematic."

Suddenly the air crackled with all sorts of male testosterone. I waved a hand to break the tension before it escalated. "We will, Detective Keeler. Neither of us wants a murderer to go free. We've always cooperated with the police, but until you have something specific to ask us, we can't just begin divulging information about clients that may have nothing at all to do with this murder."

The detective stood and shoved his pen back into his pocket, pulling out a card and slapping it on top of my desk. "If something comes up, please call me. And Mrs. Carrera? Don't go all Jessica Fletcher on me and get locked in a dumpster this time."

I flushed red and glared at his back as he left the office.

"So," J.T. drawled. "When were you going to tell me about getting into a shouting match with Spencer Thompson at the offices of Fullbright and Mason?"

CHAPTER 14

*T*hankfully, I did not lose my job over the incident at Fullbright and Mason. I spent the next few hours working on the skip traces, occasionally glancing at the paperwork Violet had given me. J.T. remained in the office, doing paperwork of his own. Finally, I couldn't take it anymore. I yanked the paperwork over to me and pulled up the bank website, using the list of usernames and passwords that Marissa Thompson had supplied to try to hack into her husband's account. On the second try I got in, but ended up with a security question to answer, no doubt because of the unfamiliar IP on the login.

What is your favorite color?

I rolled my eyes and typed in "green," thrilled that Spencer Thompson was so predictable. When I clicked on the account, my eyes nearly fell out of my head. The balance was close to a million dollars. Where the heck had Spencer Thompson gotten a million dollars? Was flipping properties that profitable? Had he really turned a few hundred dollars diverted from his savings account into this fortune? Judging from his scathing reaction to my meager savings, it was more than ironic. The guy had gone from comfortable middle class to millionaire in a scant five years. I scrolled down through the account records. No, less than five years. The account records only went back a year. The opening balance was a paltry nine thousand dollars. Over the last nine months, there were a myriad of deposits, transfers from other accounts, and what looked to be certified checks. Most of them were in increments under ten thousand, but the last two months had seen huge transfers of hundreds of thousands of dollars. But to flip houses, Spencer Thompson had to first buy them, and the checks I was seeing for purchases at foreclosure auctions and tax sales didn't make sense. I downloaded and printed everything—transaction details and copies of checks and deposits, then got out my highlighters and pen.

Five properties in the last nine months, including Melvin Elmer's. Mr. Elmer's property hadn't been sold, and assuming the other two had…

How did flipping four properties add up to a million dollars? I picked up the phone, realizing once more that I was in over my head.

"Violet? Can you come over tonight and help me? I've got check copies and transaction records, but none of this makes sense. I'm hoping you can trace the money transfers and figure out where this money came from. Give me a call back."

I hung up and turned to J.T. "There's a million dollars in this account. Do you think…maybe his wife…?"

J.T. got up and came over to look at my computer, sucking in a breath when he saw the balance. "I'm clearly in the wrong business here. Maybe I need to start telling old people what to do with their money."

"He didn't make a million dollars doing that. And I'm not even sure he made it flipping houses. Unless he's been doing it a long time and has other accounts. Or maybe an account before he opened this one? These transfers came from somewhere, and I doubt they're all escrow checks from property sales. If so, where are the checks for the original purchases?"

J.T. pointed to a sheet. "Here? These three are a foreclosure and there's a tax sale buy."

"And those two sold for nearly half a million dollars?" I laughed. "There aren't many houses in the county worth that. I think it would have been all over the paper if some local rich person lost their mansion at a tax sale for twelve thousand dollars."

"Then you're right. There must be another account besides this one. And where did he get all this money?" J.T. said, echoing my thoughts. "His wife would have noticed if he'd been siphoning tens of thousands of dollars out of their savings to fund this scheme. Where did his start-up investment come from?"

"That's the mystery," I told my boss.

"Yeah, that and who killed him." J.T. walked back to his desk. "I'm going to call Mrs. Thompson and let her know there's significant assets in this account and she should get her lawyer on it immediately."

I grimaced, thinking of our conversation this morning. If she'd had Spencer served with the divorce papers today and he'd not died, I had a feeling this account would have been closed and emptied with the guy halfway to South America. Or not. If Spencer Thompson had a lucrative business going on here, half a continuing loaf was better than none. Better to work out a deal and pay his soon-to-be ex half a million, continuing to generate money at this rate, than grab it all and end up in another country where you had to live the rest of your life on what you'd hauled down in a suitcase.

J.T. hung up the phone and shook his head. "Left a message. Do you think Marissa Thompson decided she wanted all of a million dollars instead of half?"

I shrugged. "She didn't know how much was in the account, or even where the account was. All she knew as of this morning was that her husband had a side business she'd known nothing about, and that there were probably some significant assets under that business name. She was angry. Furious. I'm thinking that maybe I wasn't the only one yelling at Spencer Thompson in his office today, but I can't see her killing him over what for all she knew might have been a few thousand dollars."

J.T. shook his head. "I don't know. If I were that detective, I'd be looking at Mrs. Thompson. Poison is a woman's weapon."

I snorted. "Maybe it is if you read a lot of mystery novels. Personally, I'd go for a knife. Or a gun. At least that way you're sure the person is dead."

"But that's messy," J.T. countered. "And it leaves you holding a murder weapon and covered either in blood or gunshot residue or both. You could be halfway across the country with an alibi using poison."

I couldn't believe we were having this discussion. "Yeah, but there's a lot of research that goes into poison. And browser history isn't as easy to delete as everyone thinks. Neither are those credit card receipts and store records that show you buying a box of rat poison a few days earlier. I still think most women would go for a gun or a knife."

"Holt got killed with drugs," he countered.

"That was accidental," I reminded him. "And Luanne Trainor took an iPad to the side of the head."

"I still think poison means it's more likely to be a woman, and Mrs. Thompson would be my top suspect."

"I'm sure Spencer Thompson angered a lot more women than me and his wife," I commented dryly. "There could still be a mistress that I haven't turned up. There could be disgruntled clients. Maybe Tracey Abramson decided

Spencer Thompson needed to go. Maybe Melvin Elmer drove down there with a box of rat poison and dumped it in the man's coffee. Maybe he grabbed the receptionist's butt one too many times, or there was a coworker that didn't get the promotion, or a manager whose wife Spencer screwed. The possibilities are endless."

J.T. chuckled, then waved at me to pack up as his phone began to ring. After a few exchanged words, he motioned for me to stay.

"That was Marissa Thompson's lawyer," he told me as he hung up the phone. "It seems Detective Keeler and I have a lot in common. He brought Mrs. Thompson in for questioning in her husband's murder. And you *weren't* the only one yelling at Mr. Thompson in his office today. It seems after speaking with you, Marissa headed over there to vent her anger at her husband for having a business on the sly. The lawyer is requesting we continue to look for accounts as well as any possible affair, and that we are free to tell the police everything we found out on his client's behalf, as well as that she knew nothing about the size of any bank accounts or anything beyond the fact that her husband was flipping properties behind her back."

I rolled my eyes. "Keeler isn't an idiot. Poisoning takes some planning. I doubt Marissa Thompson ran out of the coffee shop at eight o'clock this morning and bought poison in between our talk and her going to Fullbright and Mason. And she certainly wasn't planning on killing him before that. I don't think she was planning on killing him after that, either."

"Plus, Spencer Thompson would hardly leave his irate wife unattended in his office area so she could lace his coffee with poison," J.T. added.

"Plus, plus, if she went there right after we spoke, that means he hadn't touched his coffee for four hours. Nobody, even those with a giant mug and a warmer plate, lets their coffee sit untouched for four hours. The poisoning had to take place sometime in the hour before I got there, or right afterward."

"Fess up, Kay," J.T. teased. "You killed the guy."

I raised my hands. "I swear I'm innocent. Well, innocent of everything except losing my temper and causing a scene at Fullbright and Mason."

"Speaking of…" J.T. waggled an index finger at me. "No more of that. Professional behavior. And put our clients first. I know you want to help this old guy, but you can't let that interfere with what's paying the bills."

He was right. Although deep inside I knew that when it came to a choice between a paying client and seeing justice served, I'd lean toward the latter. Which probably meant I might not last long in this job.

I wasn't a superhero. I had bills to pay as well and being some sort of geriatric Nancy Drew wouldn't satisfy my mortgage company or put food on the table. J.T. was right. Paying clients had to be a priority. But there was nothing that said I couldn't continue to seek justice for people on my own time.

CHAPTER 15

"*J* had an idea," Violet announced as she plopped an armful of papers on my dining room table. We were on one side of the table, and Judge Beck was on the other, trying to pretend to be working while obviously listening in to our conversation.

"Spill it," I told the young woman.

"Well, tracing bank transfers and deposits without a subpoena and the bank's cooperation is a whole lot of hacking that's way out of my comfort zone and ability, so I decided to tackle this from a property title angle."

"I'm not hearing this," Judge Beck murmured. "Not hearing anything about hacking into back accounts. Not at all."

"Nobody is hacking anything," I told him. "Although I have no idea what Violet means when she says she is looking at this from a property title angle."

The girl tossed her blonde ponytail over her shoulder and sat down in the chair. "Okay, think of it this way. The bank isn't going to give us information on Brockhurst Properties' deposits without a court order, right?"

"Right."

"We've got a list of what banks initiated the transfer, and it probably won't take long for the guy's wife to get all that information since he's dead, right?"

"Marissa Thompson can authorize her lawyer to get the banking information, especially once she gets a death certificate, but that doesn't help us right now," I countered. "Melvin Elmer only has a few weeks before he's evicted."

"The only thing that will help Melvin Elmer is a lawyer," Judge Beck spoke up. "Be honest, Kay. What's the real reason you're continuing to dig into Spencer Thompson's side business?"

"Because I suspect he got the money illegally. I don't know how or from whom, but I think he embezzled it and if I track it backward far enough, I'm hoping to figure out where he stole it and get it restored to its rightful owner before Marissa Thompson runs off and buys a house in South Beach with it all," I retorted.

"So we have two goals. Or you have two goals," Judge Beck said with a smile. "One is to expose a potential embezzlement. The other is to prove identity theft and fraud. And both cases are intertwined. Is that a coincidence? Or does this linking go deeper than you've thought to date?"

His meaning hit me about the same time as it hit Violet.

"You're thinking that Spencer Thompson was the identity thief? That he took out a hundred-thousand-dollar mortgage fraudulently, then bought the house at his own foreclosure sale to flip?" Violet's mouth dropped open. "That's horrible. That's beyond predatory. He ruined that old man's life twice, then refused to even give him six months in his home. What a monster. I'm glad he's dead."

"Isn't that kind of farfetched?" I asked. "I can see Spencer Thompson padding his bank account, or stealing money from Humble Properties, LLC in some crazy accounting shell game, but identity theft and mortgage fraud? That falls in the category of people who stick skimmers in credit card machines and run phishing websites. It seems... I don't know, it seems rather crude and unsophisticated for a financial investment counselor. And risky."

"Less risky than you think," Violet told me. "A huge percentage of identity thieves are never caught. Small crimes get less attention than huge corporate embezzlements, especially when an at-risk population is targeted. It's probably a safer way to steal money that way than pad your expense account."

"I wouldn't call a hundred thousand dollars a small crime," I pointed out.

"No, but Violet is right about crimes against companies versus crimes against a vulnerable section of our population," Judge Beck said. "Corporations have the resources to come after someone with a hammer. Thousands of people with a few thousand dollars each in fake credit card charges are usually police reports that end up going nowhere."

"One hundred thousand dollars," I reminded him. "That's a felony. And a mortgage company isn't likely to take that sort of thing in stride and shrug it off."

"Which is why I called the title company," Violet told me. "*And* the mortgage company. Let's trace this at both ends and see if they meet in the middle. I agree with Judge Beck. I'm thinking Spencer Thompson figured he could rip off elderly people with no real support system and no assets to fight back. Just think, if you hadn't gone to visit Melvin Elmer this week, he would have moved out and Spencer Thompson would have flipped that house for a big profit. Double profit if he was the one that pocketed that hundred-thousand-dollar loan."

"And the mortgage company would cooperate with us

before the bank would?" I asked. "I would have thought you'd have needed a court order for that as well."

Violet shot me a mischievous smile. "No one wants to receive a call from a county tax assessor's office stating that they've received a fraud complaint from a homeowner. Worse, the title company that did the transfer to Spencer Thompson from the foreclosure sale is on the hook, too. I made sure to call them first, knowing they'd be on the phone in five seconds with the mortgage company, holding them accountable for asserting a fraudulent lien. In less than an hour I had two angry title companies with mud on their faces, and one panicked mortgage company that was kind enough to send me this."

She shoved a piece of paper across the table to me and I read it, Judge Beck eyeing it over my shoulder.

"I'd strike the eviction based on this," the judge commented. "And if Spencer Thompson was still alive, I'd tell him I didn't want to see him in my courtroom again until this matter was resolved and he could prove a clear title to the home."

I beamed. "Thank you, Violet. I still want to see justice done as far as this identity theft, and any potential embezzlement from Spencer Thompson, but this takes one huge worry off my shoulders."

The memo on official mortgage company letterhead stated that due to questions concerning the validity of the loan and title, they were in the process of conducting an internal investigation and would notify all interested parties of the results. It was addressed to Brockhurst Properties, the two title companies, Melvin Elmer, and the county Records Division. I'd been thinking lots of bad thoughts about the mortgage company and their sloppy loan origination practices, but this memo and their quick response to Violet's call gave me hope that they weren't all just sharks looking to make a buck.

"There's one other thing I found." Violet slid me another stack of papers.

"You're not paying this young woman enough," Judge Beck said as we read through them. "And you, Miss Smith, should have gone to law school."

Violet beamed in response.

"So, these are all the homes owned by Brockhurst Properties in the last three years?"

She nodded. "Yes. The first six were Humble-House-owned, sold to their for-profit company, then re-sold to Brockhurst Properties who flipped them at closing to the buyer."

I shook my head, still not understanding all this paperwork. "Flipped at closing? Why?"

"To get a cut of the profits—a cut that Tracey Abramson is probably unaware of." Violet bounced in her chair, her grin huge. "See, Humble House acquires the title through one of their programs, and when the owner dies, they sell it at a minor profit to their side company as a distressed property."

"I know. Tracey Abramson told me all this and while it sounds shady as heck, I've been told it's all above board."

"As long as it's not too far under market value, yes. Eighty percent is usually the rule, but market value is a tricky thing and appraisals can come in however you want them. Humble House gets a low appraisal, sells to their for-profit wing at eighty percent of that, then the other company gets a new appraisal based on 'improvements' and sells for a significant profit."

"Then why the transfer at closing to Brockhurst?" I asked, shaking my head in confusion. By this point, Judge Beck had abandoned any pretense of doing work and was listening intently to our conversation.

"It's a money grab." Violet flipped a piece of paper over and began writing down numbers. "Let's say Humble House clears thirty thousand in profit. The second appraisal comes in and Humble Properties, LLC sells the property. But there's a third appraisal that's what the actual buyer is paying, and it's got an extra thirty thousand built into it. Rather than have Humble Properties, LLC clear eighty thousand, Spencer Thompson uses the second appraisal. He lets the LLC take fifty thousand in profit and sells to Brockhurst Properties, then immediately, as in within an hour immediately, sells to the actual buyer for thirty thousand more. Brockhurst Properties never needs to front the cash, because it's all handled by the title company in escrow and it never shows on the actual title because the sale is at closing. Humble House, i.e. Tracey Abramson, would never realize what happened. For all he knows, Brockhurst Properties is an investment company, an REIT handling single-family home rentals. If they buy six of their assets and the purchase looks good as far as the second appraisal goes, it wouldn't cause any red flags. Spencer Thompson double dips on each sale, and no one is the wiser."

"Yes, you definitely aren't paying her enough," Judge Beck repeated. "And is the county tax assessment office aware of her talent? Screw that, is the prosecutor's office aware of her talent?"

"I'd be thrilled if you wrote me a recommendation, Judge Beck," Violet told him, her face pink at his praise. "Or if you mentioned my name to anyone looking to hire a forensic accountant who minored in cyber security."

"But wait." I waved a hand to get us back on topic. Not that I wanted to downplay Violet's brilliance or her untapped talent, but I was worried that if I got distracted, I'd lose my very fragile understanding of the situation. "There's an issue here. Tracey Abramson *isn't* unaware of Spencer Thompson's double dipping. He's the one who had me look into Brock-hurst Properties. And he said he was shutting down the for-profit side of the company as well as refusing to sell it to Spencer Thompson. I think he was very much aware of what was going on, at least in the last week."

"That would be why the Humble Properties, LLC flips stopped at six." Violet pointed down at the papers. "These last ten weren't flips at closing. Spencer Thompson needed cash up front to buy these at tax and foreclosure sales. I can see the first three or four being funded from what he'd skimmed from Humble House, but in the last nine months, he'd must have started to have a cash flow issue. You can process title and resell a property only so quickly."

"And that's when you think he started to do his identity theft," I added.

"Yes. I think he got greedy, saw some opportunities that were too good to pass by, and no longer had Humble House to rely upon, so he turned to something else."

"I don't know, Violet." I shook my head. "I think that's where you jump the shark."

She blinked at the unfamiliar reference, but Judge Beck chuckled.

"You two are amazing. Like Sherlock and Watson, only much better looking."

"And without the cocaine habit," I added.

"Am I Watson?" Violet teased. "Or is Kay supposed to be Watson?"

"Detective Keeler thinks I'm Jessica Fletcher," I told her, "so you be Sherlock on this case."

"Maybe you can both be Sherlock without the cocaine habit," Judge Beck said. "Either way, I'm impressed. This is far more interesting than these motions I brought home to go over tonight."

I was sure it was, but although Violet had made significant progress, we still had no idea who had killed Spencer Thompson. Was it his wife, wanting all the money instead of half, or worried that her husband's risky behavior was going to cost them everything financially? Was it Tracey Abramson, angered at how Spencer Thompson had betrayed his trust and filtered their LLC profits into another company for his sole gain? Or was it someone else who had a grudge against the man? Honestly, anyone could have been the murderer, from a dying Melvin Elmer to a disgruntled client. Anyone.

CHAPTER 16

"*W*hy not? Matt Poffenberger is a good--looking guy. You like him. He likes you. Get naked and get busy," Daisy announced the next morning at yoga. She'd been telling me about how J.T. had given her an adorable cat mug as a gift the other day, and how excited she was about their dinner this weekend at Etienne's, and that had somehow transitioned into her deciding I needed to date—no, *more* than date—Matt Poffenberger.

I sputtered, nearly toppling from my triangle pose. "Daisy! Matt and I are friends. We're not dating."

I'd made the mistake of telling Daisy that I was slightly envious of her budding relationship with J.T., and now she was busy playing matchmaker.

"Pfft. So don't date him then. Be friends with benefits. That's the joy of not being twenty anymore. No worries about commitments, or them calling you the next day, or whether they're going to spread it around the school that you did it with them. Just sex between two consenting adults who like and respect each other. How cool is that?"

"Daisy…" But she was on a roll and there was no stopping my friend now.

"He doesn't even have to buy you dinner or anything. Or spend the night, because that might be awkward with Judge Beck and the kids here. You set the rules. You probably don't even need to fret over birth control, unless you're like me and your ovaries just won't get the message that they need to shut it down and call it a day. Just hot, no-strings-attached sex."

"I don't want hot, no-strings-attached sex," I told her. Although the idea did have a strange kind of appeal in a naughty fantasy sort of way. But no. I was mortified just thinking about it. And coming from my friend, who was giggly over a chaste kiss with the man she'd been dating for the last month, this seemed a bit over the top.

Daisy grinned at me. "I'd do Matt, but he's not the slightest bit interested in me. Go for it, Kay."

"I am most certainly not going to go for it." I tried to straighten my back and look both outraged and dignified. "Matt is my friend, and that's it. I'm grieving. And even if I wasn't, I'm hardly going to be getting it on with Judge Beck and his kids living here."

Daisy's eyebrows shot up. "Oh, Judge Beck. That's how the land lies, huh? Can't say I blame you. He's gorgeous."

"He's in the middle of a messy divorce," I retorted. "And I'm twenty years older than he is. And we're just friends. Cut it out, Daisy. This isn't funny."

Daisy got that shrewd look on her face. "You're more like fifteen years older than he is. And in spite of your weird knitting obsession, you're not old."

"Stop trying to set me up with my roommate and every other man over the age of thirty you know," I hissed at her.

Daisy rolled her eyes. "Fine. But at least let me drag you

to the spa this weekend. Mani/pedi, a facial, and a cut and color on your hair. My treat."

I longed for a spa day, but I had plans. "I can't. We're going to see Madison's cross-country meet on Saturday, then going out for pizza."

"If I didn't know any better, I'd think those were your step kids." Daisy shifted into an Utthita Parsvakonasana.

"I like to think of myself as their adopted grandmother," I told her, mirroring her pose.

She snorted. "Grandmother, my ass. Stop acting like you've got one foot in the grave, Kay. You're an attractive woman. You're smart and fun. Those kids adore you. Five minutes after he moved in, Judge Beck is considering you one of his best friends. And that, Matt Poffenberger gives you big ole puppy dog eyes every month at bingo. How many times have you gone out to lunch with him? How many times have you gone over to visit his father? How many of his charity events are you fundraising for?"

"A lot," I confessed. "But he's just a friend, Daisy. Eli passed away six months ago. I'm not ready. I'm still in mourning."

I still see his ghost is what I wanted to add. Daisy knew I saw ghosts, but I hadn't talked to her about the one that followed me from room to room each night. The one that set up watch in my bedroom as I slept. The one whose presence was a constant comfort to me. Although I'd begun to feel a bit guilty that sometimes I didn't even notice he was there, that so many times I didn't even think about him.

Six months. How could I possibly be starting to move on after only six months? How could I possibly ever consider loving another man when Eli had been the love of my life, my soul mate, my until death do we part?

Until death do we part. Oh, God.

"Well, you aren't going to be eating pizza all day. If I make our spa appointments for three, will you be back by then? Or on Sunday?"

I bit my lip, following Daisy into our eagle pose. "I'm assuming I'll be back by then. Maybe make the appointment for four?"

"Four it is." She shot me a stern look. "And you're getting your hair done. Nails. Feet. Hair. The works, girl."

"Okay, but I'm not *dyeing* my hair. I don't want to be one of those old women with the fake-looking black hair. I'm owning my gray. It's who I am."

"Can't you own your gray with highlights?" Daisy said, shifting into a low lunge.

I glanced at Daisy's platinum blonde hair as I mirrored her pose. It looked good on her—edgy and stylish. There was no way I could pull that off. "I don't want to be one of those old women with the floozy-blonde hair, either."

"I'm not saying you need to go crazy. Just some warm blonde foils. Trust me."

I eyed her, not sure if my trust for my best friend extended to letting her "foil" my hair. "So streaks, only a dark gold-blonde instead of white? I don't want to be all stripy-headed."

"Foils. They can do super light blonde, but I think you'd look better with more of a gold tone."

I took a deep breath. "Okay. In full disclosure, I haven't colored my hair in almost forty years."

Daisy chuckled. "Forty years? Good grief, Kay. Did they even have hair dye back then? Did you just smear crushed berries on your head or something?"

"Ha, ha. Actually, back in the day, we called it frosting, not foils," I said.

"Well, this isn't the same as forty years ago," Daisy told me. "For one thing, they don't slap a plastic cap on your head and yank chunks of hair through it with an oversized crochet hook."

Which hadn't been too bad when the person getting the highlights had short hair. I winced, remembering the beautician pulling my long, permed hair through the holes in that cap. Yikes. I was lucky I even had hair after all the chemical processing I'd put my scalp through back then. But the frosting *had* looked good. My ash-toned brown hair had appeared sun-kissed with the frosted blonde streaks in the permed curls. Then I'd turned twenty-two and didn't have money for perms, let alone frosting. By the time Eli and I were married and he was a doctor and earning enough money to consider having a professional touch my hair, I'd decided big hair wasn't my thing. Trims at the local beauty school had been a bargain. And the last ten years, I'd cut it myself, not even able to justify the expense of the beauty school. Yes, it probably was time for me to have someone who knew what they were doing cut and color my hair.

And don't get me started on nails and feet.

"Then after we're done, we'll call up Matt Poffenberger and have him meet us for drinks. Bet he'll be bowled over by how gorgeous you are with your foils and snazzy manicure."

I bit back a smile, thinking that after the week I'd had, a little spa pampering and a bit of male admiration would go a long way. My first investigation case. A whole lot of unsavory business practices. Identity theft and an elderly man being evicted from his home. And the possibility that the villain in this scenario might be the dead man. Made me think whoever killed him deserved my sympathy as opposed to justice.

"Happy hour on the porch tonight?" Daisy asked, moving us into the child's pose that signaled the end of our morning yoga. I could already taste the coffee and the cinnamon raisin rolls I'd made the night before.

"Yes, happy hour. I've got a bottle of Pinot chilling in the fridge as we speak."

"Good." Daisy stood up and stretched tall, her hands reaching toward the sky. "I've got a bottle of my own to contribute. I think the Tennisons might come down to join us."

I turned to her in surprise. "The Tennisons?" They were a trust-fund couple with more money then I'd imagined possible, and they were also the couple that had the most picture--perfect house and garden on the street.

"The Tennisons." She grinned at me and headed for the house. "Now let's go get some coffee and whatever you baked last night and get going. I hear you've got a murder to solve?"

I snorted. "Detective Keeler has a murder to solve. I've got six skip traces to do and the findings of an investigation to type up along with an invoice."

But she was right. I might not be the one in charge of solving Spencer Thompson's murder, but I did have information I needed to deliver to Detective Keeler—information that might help him arrest the killer.

CHAPTER 17

I plopped a stack of copies down in front of Detective Keeler and sat in the narrow, uncomfortable chair beside his desk. "Spencer Thompson was moonlighting. Twice. Once in a partnership gone sour with Tracey Abramson, and once in a company of his own that flipped properties."

Now that we had the okay from Marissa Thompson and her lawyer to divulge all this to law enforcement, I was singing like a canary. Or a crow.

Detective Keeler shot me a sour look. "You're telling me he was killed in a real estate deal gone bad?"

"One of the companies was co-owned by Tracey Abramson who owns the Humble House foundation. Turns out that Spencer Thompson was his partner and they didn't part on good terms. Abramson has been trying to buy the business out from Thompson for the last year and close it down, but Thompson has been holding out on him. I'd gone to talk to Abramson and he pointed me to Thompson's secondary business, telling me to look into it."

The expression on Keeler's face remained unchanged.

"So, you're thinking Tracey Abramson killed Spencer Thompson, but told you about their disagreements and the name of Thompson's new company first?"

I winced at the derision in the detective's voice. "Maybe he wasn't planning on killing him at first but having me expose what his new company was doing. Then he discovered Thompson's business practices weren't just unsavory, but actually involved embezzlement, and killed him instead."

The man eyed me over the rim of his glasses. The silence extended for an uncomfortably long time. "And you have proof of this embezzlement?"

I tapped the title documentation. "He was getting lowball appraisals for the properties, then selling them to himself and flipping them at the closing table for a profit. When I met with Tracey Abramson, he told me he thought Thompson was too aggressive and that the LLC was going to hurt the reputation of his non-profit. I don't think he knew about the double-dipping."

"And you're saying that he discovered the embezzlement within the last few days? And he knew about this Brockhurst Properties, and knew there was something shady about that?"

I nodded. "So Tracey Abramson definitely has motive. And opportunity. And probably means. I'm assuming anyone can buy a box of rat poison."

"I can hardly see Tracey Abramson murdering by rat poison," the detective commented dryly. "He's more of the hire-a-hitman stereotype, don't you think?"

"He's just as good of a suspect as the wife," I shot back.

His eyebrows went up and he tapped the stack of copies. "You're saying that Spencer Thompson had a ton of money in private and business accounts, all of which the estranged wife stood to inherit upon his death, but she's not a good suspect?"

I felt my face heat up. "I'm saying Tracey Abramson is just a good a suspect. I don't think Marissa Thompson is guilty of her husband's murder."

He tapped the stack again. "She was there in his office, yelling at him about three hours before you came in, and stood to inherit a lot of money upon his death."

"Poison requires planning. It's not a heat-of-the-moment, yelling-in-the-office kind of murder," I shot back. "I doubt Marissa Thompson carries rat poison around in her purse. And I doubt her husband let his coffee sit there on his desk for three hours before taking a sip."

He blinked. I felt somewhat vindicated as he leaned back in his chair and regarded me.

"Poisoning is a woman's method of murder. And it wasn't rat poison. It was a botanical."

I absorbed that bit of new information and regrouped.

"Well, I doubt she was carrying a foxglove plant around in her purse, either. The fact that Spencer Thompson was killed by a botanical agent in his coffee proves that this took a lot of planning and preparation. That's not the sort of killer that's going to bring notice to *himself* by yelling at the intended victim in front of his entire office full of coworkers." I purposely emphasized the gendered pronoun, stung that the detective as well as my boss were insisting the killer was female simply due to the method used.

"I'll look into Tracey Abramson," Detective Keeler grudgingly informed me. "But I doubt he's our killer."

I huffed, thinking the detective was very narrow minded.

"So tell me about this Brockhurst Properties." He sat back up in his chair and began looking through the stack of copies. Progress. At least he was taking me seriously and not dumping the whole batch in the trash and showing me the door.

"When things went south with Tracey Abramson and he

was being pushed out of their partnership, Spencer Thompson started Brockhurst Properties to continue his real estate flipping. But the problem quickly became cash flow. He had enough to buy the first few houses but couldn't move them fast enough to free up cash for additional purchases. Somehow, he's getting the money to buy these other houses, and it's not coming from personal assets."

"You think he's stealing."

"Yes. Specifically, we...I mean, I... suspect he might be using identity fraud to take out fake mortgages on these homes, buying them at the foreclosure sale with the money he got from the mortgage, then flipping them."

"Doesn't sound like the sort of thing a smart man who has been successfully running a scam on his partner would do."

"I think it's a short-term strategy to build up enough money to fund his real estate investments and possibly buy out Tracey Abramson. I don't think he intended it as a long-term thing. And I think he's got a partner on the inside." I pointed to the papers. "Peabody Mortgage underwrote all these loans, all to different lenders."

"And why should I look into this? It's hard to prosecute a dead man, you know."

"It's still a crime," I insisted. "Identity theft. Mortgage fraud. And it's possible that someone at Peabody needed Spencer to die."

His eyebrows went up. "So somebody at Peabody Mortgage drove from..." he looked at the papers, "from Philadelphia, just so he could poison Spencer Thompson's coffee?"

Well, when he put it that way, it didn't seem very plausible. "It might have happened. There was an emergency. They were about to get caught. The guy hauls down here to meet with Spencer Thompson, but it doesn't go well—"

"And he runs outside, clips some leaves off the landscaping, and runs back in the office to dump them in Spencer Thompson's coffee when his back is turned."

This sounded a lot better when I'd thought it was rat poison, or even an overdose of blood pressure medication. Maybe the key to who killed Spencer Thompson wasn't motive, it was means. The type of poison used had to be a limiting factor in all this.

"What kind of botanical was it?" I asked, my mind whirling. There was a lot of information someone could gain over the internet regarding poisonous plants, but knowing how to identify the correct shrub, which parts to harvest, how to process it safely, and how much to use would take more than a quick afternoon's search.

"We won't know that until the lab results get back. It was clearly a botanical because there were traces of crushed, dried flowers and leaves at the bottom of the coffee cup. The woman in the office with Spencer Thompson said at first she thought he was having an allergic reaction to something. He was clutching his chest like he couldn't breathe, but also spitting. He stumbled and fell to the floor and began having spasms."

I frowned. "Maybe it was an allergic reaction to something."

"No allergies according to his medical records, his friends or coworkers, or his wife. And the M.E. said Thompson had severe blistering to the soft tissues of his mouth and throat and mucus membranes, as well as his upper digestive tract. Someone poisoned his coffee. And that someone knew exactly what they were doing."

"And Spencer Thompson didn't notice a bunch of dried flowers and leaves floating around in his beverage?" Now I was the skeptic, eyeing Detective Keeler with raised eyebrows.

"There were just a few bits and they were tiny. The M.E.

believes that whatever plant it was, the killer crushed them and basically used the 'juice.' The small amount of debris in the bottom of the cup were probably remnants of the distillation process and not delivering the actual poison dosage."

"And you seriously can see Marissa Thompson distilling plant bits in a pot in her kitchen?" I asked incredulously.

"You can see Tracey Abramson doing that?"

Good point. Tracey Abramson would have hired a hit man and had an ironclad alibi. Thompson wouldn't have died by poison. He would have just vanished, only to be found three years from now chained to some cement blocks at the bottom of a lake.

"Besides, Tracey Abramson isn't on the list." Detective Keeler slid a photo over to me. It showed the visitor's log from the receptionist desk, with little notes about which employee the visitors were seeing. My name was on there toward the bottom. Marissa Thompson's was on there close to the top. And in between were five other unfamiliar names.

"So unless Tracey Abramson hired one of these people," the detective continued, "then he's not our murderer."

Our. I looked up at Keeler with a puzzled frown. "Why are you showing me all this? I thought you weren't big on sharing information about cases, especially to a Jessica Fletcher wannabe."

He chuckled. "You know, that old lady solved a lot of cases. And you seem to have a pretty good track record yourself. Pickford speaks highly of you."

"Miles likes that I supply him with muffins, cookies, and scones." I laughed.

"Can't fault a man for that. You make one mean muffin, Mrs. Carrera. And as wild as some of your theories are, you clearly have either connections or methods of research that aren't available to me. Well, aren't available to me without getting eight signatures on a budget request and waiting three months for approvals."

"So, we're working together now?" I stuck out my hand.

He eyed it and leaned back in his chair. "No, we're not *working together*. Consider this a temporary cooperation because I'm definitely wanting to be in the loop on anything else you dig up on this case, and I get the feeling you're not going to be so willing to share that information with me unless I'm a bit forthcoming on my own here."

I lowered my hand and stood. "Don't be silly, Detective Keeler. I just want to see justice being served."

He turned to his computer, clearly dismissing me. "Then go help me serve justice, Mrs. Carrera."

I headed into the office, letting J.T. know all the juicy details I'd discovered last night thanks to Violet and her diligence. Then I typed up all the details including the bank account number and copies of all the paperwork Violet had given me, added up my hours into an invoice and turned it all over to J.T. by lunchtime.

The rest of the afternoon was spent doing skip traces, which were blissfully familiar and almost meditative in their monotony compared to the Thompson case. It made me wish for the time when I hadn't had my investigator's license and had just sat a computer all day, tracking down those who defaulted on their loans. By five o'clock, I felt downright relaxed as I finished up my work, packed my laptop and a few files I might want to review over the weekend, and headed home.

The weekend. Happy hour on the porch. Madison's cross-country meet. A spa day with Daisy, and maybe, just maybe I'd finish that scarf I'd been working on for the last few weeks.

A blissful weekend. I couldn't wait.

CHAPTER 18

"More wine?" Daisy started pouring before I'd even nodded. We had quite the crew here for our happy hour on my front porch. Lars and Kat were over, chatting with the Tennisons about the likelihood of getting the pothole on our street fixed before winter set in. Bert Peter was taking a break from the never-ending job of sorting through the contents of his late uncle's house across the street. Olive was here straight from work in her business suit, briefcase propped against my porch railing as she cradled her wine in one hand and gestured wildly with the other. Suzette was nodding in agreement with her, occasionally chiming in about the difficulty of finding quality accounting clerks to replace interns returning to college. Violet had even come by, standing shyly off to the side and cradling her untouched glass of Chardonnay as she listened in on Olive and Suzette's conversation. I'd introduced the young woman when she arrived, and hoped for her to make some friends, or at the very least connections she could use when trying for her next job. Judge Beck was right. Her talents really were wasted at the county tax assessor's office.

All she needed was for someone to see her ability under the shiny new college degree and scant job experience and give her a chance.

"Whoa," I told Daisy as she continued far past the halfway point on my wine glass. "I've got some work to do tonight. Passing out on the couch at six isn't in my schedule."

My friend scrunched up her nose but pulled the bottle away. "It's Friday night, Kay! I don't like you working late all the time like this. I don't like you ducking out of our morning yoga early, either. Am I gonna have to have a talk with your boss?"

I grinned, liking that my friend seemed to relish her power over my "boss." "Do not screw up my new promotion," I told her. "And technically it's not work anymore. We've pretty much done all we can do for our client. Right now, I'm trying to figure out a murder. And help someone not get evicted from his home, although I think that's taken care of."

I did want to get Melvin Elmer hooked up with a lawyer, though. Yes, he was dying, but I hated the thought that some slimeball of an identity thief had caused him all this grief and was getting away with a hundred grand of his home equity.

"Another murder." Daisy added a splash of wine to her own glass, then took a quick drink. "What's happening to our little town? First that party planner, then poor Mr. Peter, then Holt Dupree, then Luanne Trainor. Things are getting out of hand. Lay off the murder. Someone needs to burn down a building or kidnap a dog or something."

"No, someone does not need to commit arson or steal a dog," I retorted. "And not all those murders were in Locust Point. Luanne was murdered in Milford, and Holt was technically outside the town limits when he died."

"Still, that's a whole lot of foul play in six months. I assume you're talking about that investment guy? I heard his wife offed him for the money. What's to investigate?"

"I'm pretty sure she didn't do it. This wasn't a heat-of-the-moment crime. Someone planned this out and took a lot of care with it."

"Mistress? Business rival? Someone he cut off in traffic earlier that morning?" Daisy took another sip of wine. "Do tell, Detective Carrera. Who do you think did the deed?"

"Well, the person I had as my primary suspect doesn't seem too likely after I found out the method of murder," I confessed. "It would have taken a specific sort of knowledge and a lot of forethought, and that doesn't seem like the method he'd go for. Or the wife either, for that matter."

"You can't just leave me hanging with that," Daisy protested. "I'm imagining all sorts of things. Beheaded with an ancient katana? Slowly devoured by ants only found in the depths of the Amazon jungle? Catapulted into the highway at rush hour?"

"No!" I laughed. "It's not public knowledge. I probably shouldn't tell anyone."

Daisy rolled her eyes. "Oh, come on. I can keep a secret. And it will probably be all over the papers tomorrow anyway."

She was right about the papers, but not about her ability to keep a secret. Daisy was a horrible gossip, although she *was* good about keeping personal stuff private.

"Okay, okay. It was poison. A botanical. I know the effects, but not what it was. We won't know that until the labs come back, and I might not know that until it goes to trial unless Detective Keeler is in a sharing kind of mood."

"A botanical?" Daisy shook her head in disbelief. "Like plants? Like strychnine-flavored romaine in his salad or something?"

I shrugged. "I really don't know plants beyond the herbs in my garden and some flowers. I know there are things like foxglove that used to be used in poisons. I know there are a lot of toxic wild plants like pokeberries, but not what might be used to kill someone."

"Ask Dora," Daisy urged.

"Dora Tennison?" I turned to look at the woman and her husband talking with Lars and Kat.

"No, Dora the Explorer." Daisy rolled her eyes. "Yes, Dora Tennison. She's a Master Gardener. Have you seen her yard?"

It was my turn to roll my eyes. "Just because she's a genius with roses doesn't mean she knows toxic plants. Unless you're implying Dora Tennison killed Spencer Thompson?"

"If Dora Tennison needed a financial advisor, she'd go to whoever is managing that trust fund she and Phil have been living off of for the last forty years, not some Fullbright and Mason dude working in a cubicle down in Milford. She's not all about roses, you know. She and Suzette go hunting mushrooms together every spring. Ginseng, too. And she taught a seminar to those survivalist whack jobs last fall on how to gather food after the zombie apocalypse or something. The woman knows her plants."

Huh. Guess I needed to chat with Dora Tennison. The awkward thing was that I barely knew the woman. Yes, she was on my porch with her husband drinking wine, but that was because I'd made it a point to invite everyone on the street. She and Phil lived a few houses down from the Larses, and as Daisy had said, even though they were my age, they were both trust fund people with abundant free time and not much in common with me. Actually, I'd made a lot of assumptions based on their immaculate lawn, immaculate house, and immaculate six-figure cars in the garage that they didn't have a lot in common with me, but maybe those assumptions were wrong. Kat Lars was pretty cool and they seemed thick as thieves over there talking together. And she couldn't be too stuffy if she went hunting for mushrooms and ginseng with Suzette and offered seminars to survivalist preppers.

I made my way over to them, hovering around the edge of their conversation and feeling a bit like Violet at the moment.

"Kay has an herb garden," Kat announced, giving me a quick smile. "Not that size of yours, Dora, but just as lovely. You should have her show it to you."

Yes, because the Master Gardener really wanted to see my scraggly thyme and lanky oregano.

"Just some kitchen herbs," I told her. "Nothing special. I added catnip this year for Taco."

"Oh, I bet he loves that. Do you have any flowering plants?" Dora smiled at me. She was really a lovely woman, but as intimidating as the Queen of England. Her snow-white hair was in an elegant French twist, her makeup as impeccable as her understated but clearly expensive pantsuit. "Your back yard would be perfect for a native-plant wild-flower garden, or perhaps some heirloom roses with a chalk-stone pathway."

I winced, thinking of the impatiens that tended to die almost as quickly as I bought them. "I have a few herbs and flowers. I'm still trying to figure out what's going to thrive in my back yard with the soil and the partial shade."

I continued to listen as Kat and Dora spoke of rose varieties, waiting for an opportunity to shift the conversation. Finally realizing that I'd be waiting forever, I just blurted it out.

"Dora? I was hoping to ask you some questions about toxic plants."

There. That wasn't awkward. Not at all. Both women turned to me with surprised expressions.

"Goodness!" Dora exclaimed. "Has Taco gotten into something he shouldn't?"

"No, something came up at work and Daisy said you knew a lot about plants that might be poisonous to humans."

"So many are," Dora told me. "I just gave a talk to one of the Boy Scout troops on toxic berries. Some are non-toxic, but things like horse nettle fruit or holly berries are better left for the birds and deer."

"I was thinking more like poisonous rather than just toxic," I told her. "As in fatal to a grown man if ingested in a concentrated form, like in a tea or extracted juice."

Kat laughed. "Judge Beck get on your wrong side, Kay? Don't kill him. He's the best--looking man on our street. Well, besides Will, that is," she added with a quick smile toward her husband. I was glad to see them getting along. There was a time a few months ago when I truly feared for their marriage. I knew they probably still had issues to work through, but the affection in her glance was promising.

"No need to fear," I told her. "I've got no plans to do away with Judge Beck, or anyone else, for that matter. I'm just researching for a case."

"Well, then, let me help you." Dora raised her wine glass. "How dead do you need this man to be? Some plants would require repeated dosing to build up the level to the point where death is feasible. Others are more fast acting, although many have enough of a window that unless the victim is out in the woods, hours away from a hospital and medical attention, he'll have a high chance of recovering."

"I pretty much want instant death," I told her. "Within a few minutes. And I'm guessing it needs to be something fairly common, not indigenous only to a remote region of Asia where the killer would need to order it off the internet."

She nodded. "Nightshade berries? They look a lot like blueberries and ingesting as little as a handful can kill someone. Or pokeweed, although he'd have to eat quite a lot of them for it to be fatal."

I thought back on my conversation with Detective Keeler. "There would be tiny fragments of leaves and flowers, but the poison would be administered in a liquid form, so something that could be boiled into a tea or pressed and the oil or juice used?"

"Hmmm. Rhododendron? The leaves look a lot like bay leaves, and a tea brewed from them can be deadly. You'd need quite a lot though, and the smell is horrible. I can't imagine someone unwittingly ingesting enough to die, because it's so foul."

I was beginning to wonder how Dora Tennison knew all this. Maybe there was a dark side to the cheerful, well-put-together, silver-haired woman.

"Poison administered through coffee," I told her. "Would a strong, dark roast be enough to cover up the taste?"

She chuckled. "No. Not Rhododendron, anyway. Hmm, does the intended victim have any allergies we could play on? Any medications to interact with? Mostly it's the fruits that are deadly, but some plants have leaves that cause respiratory distress. Someone with a compromised lung system might possibly die from that."

"No. No allergies or medicines to interact with. Healthy thirty-year-old male. The murderer needs to be fairly certain the victim is going to die, and it needs to act quickly enough that by the time the paramedics get there, he's already dead."

"Cyanide?" Kat volunteered. "You can get that from cherry pits, can't you?"

Dora nodded. "Wild cherry pits and leaves have trace amounts of cyanide, but the volume you'd need to process to get enough cyanide to kill someone is daunting. There are easier ways to do someone in."

"*Coffee* as the delivery mechanism?" Kat's husband Will had joined the conversation. "That's criminal. What sort of monster poisons someone using their morning Joe?"

"A monster who found her husband cheating?" Kat teased. "So you better watch your step, buster!"

"How about Jimson weed?" Dora's husband, Phil, asked. "Your presentation to the survivalists said as little as half a teaspoon of crushed seeds could cause death by cardiac arrest. And Jimson weed is commonly found. If I wanted to kill someone, I'd crush the seeds and add them to the coffee grounds. The coffee would mask the bitter taste and thirty minutes later, bam! Heart attack. And our local M.E. would probably never suspect anything, especially if the victim had an underlying heart condition."

Yes, I was beginning to worry about my neighbors.

"But the victim is only thirty and in good health," Olive countered. It seemed the rest of the porch happy-hour crowd had clustered around us to join the conversation. "Not the sort of guy likely to have a heart attack."

"And lacing the coffee grounds would target more than just the one person in an office with a shared coffee maker," Daisy chimed in. "Our killer only wants one person to die, not half the office."

"Ah, a killer with ethics and morals." Kat grinned. "Got it."

"Exactly," Daisy replied. "Besides, if six people in an office suddenly came down with cardiac symptoms, the M.E. would definitely suspect foul play."

"True," Phil added. "I guess my method of murder would work best in someone's home, in their house coffee maker, as long as they had the old school kind and not the newfangled ones with the little pods. Oh, and if they had a maid that would come in that evening and clean the dishes and coffee pot before anyone was the wiser, that would be a bonus."

"Remind me never to upset you, dear," Dora told him with a pat on his shoulder.

"Cardiac arrest won't work," I told them. "The death needs to present initially like an allergic reaction," I said, thinking back to what Detective Keeler had told me. "Severe respiratory distress, falling to the floor and having spasms. But it burns and blisters soft tissues—mouth, throat, mucus membranes. Causes severe gastrointestinal distress."

"Ah." Dora tapped a pink nail against her equally pink lips. "Perhaps a concentrated poison ivy oil? Urushoil is the clear liquid on and in the plant that causes the blister-like lesions. It would be fairly easy to distill down to a concentrated form, although there would be a delayed reaction. The inflammation isn't immediate."

I frowned, thinking this was far more difficult than I'd imagined. Maybe I should wait for the toxicology report after all.

"Buttercup."

We all turned at Suzette's voice. She was standing between Olive and Violet, a thoughtful expression on her face.

"Buttercup?" Daisy asked her. "That stuff is everywhere. They use it in the highway median. It's in fields. It's in just about every wildflower garden I've seen in my life. Buttercup is poisonous?"

Suzette wrinkled her nose. "I don't really know. Gran always said to keep it away from the horses. Most of them wouldn't touch the stuff, but we had this crazy pony that was on a restricted diet because of Cushing's and he'd eat pretty much any weed he found in the field. We nearly lost him one year to buttercup toxicity. He had blisters on his lips and gums, swelling on his face and colic. Would it do the same thing to humans, I wonder?"

Dora nodded. "There are hundreds of varieties of buttercups, but most of them are at the very most a skin irritant when the leaves are crushed. The sap can cause dermatitis and can also cause blistering of the mucus membranes and intestines if ingested. I guess something like tall buttercup,

Ranunculus acris, would deliver the symptoms you've described and could be fatal if enough of the sap was added to the coffee. It's got an acrid taste, but a strong dark roast would mask that enough for the victim to drink a good bit of it."

"And the effect is immediate?" I asked.

"Oh, yes, if it's the sap, definitely. It wouldn't be my choice of alkaloid, though. You might also consider monks hood, Delphinium, baneberry, or larkspur. They're all highly toxic and would cause the same reaction. Of course, none of those is quite as common in this area as tall buttercup, but someone with a love of flower gardens might grow larkspur or Delphinium."

I frowned in thought. "So, if I had a garden with tall buttercup or any of those other plants, I could crush them and gather the sap into some sort of vial, then add it to someone's dark roast coffee and kill them."

"Oh, yes," Dora Tennison said with an angelic smile. "You most definitely could kill them."

* * *

"I'm so glad it's the weekend."

I'd ditched the work I'd brought home with me and was curled up on the couch, knitting and listening to Styx vinyl on the old console that Henry had refurbished. Judge Beck was opposite me in the huge recliner, reading a book, Taco curled up on his lap. It was midnight. I'd been somewhat buzzed from the porch happy hour and the judge had thankfully taken on dinner preparation, grilling up burgers and tossing a salad while Daisy and I finished off the wine and laughed on the porch. We'd all had dinner—the judge, the kids, Daisy, and I—then we'd headed for the hot tub and relaxed and talked about the kids' sports while the sun went down. Daisy had meandered off toward her home. The kids had headed up to bed. And the judge and I had curled up in the parlor with our various activities to herald in the weekend.

"Me, too." The judge lowered his book and eyed me over the top of his glasses. "Kay?"

"Mmm?" I finished the row on the scarf and paused.

"I...I... oh, never mind." He shifted in his chair and Taco opened his eyes and purred.

I don't know if it was the wine I'd drunk earlier, or the crazy stressful week I'd had, or the conversation that Daisy and I had this morning, but somehow all my happy feelings spilled out.

"I can't wait to go with you all to see Madison's cross-country meet tomorrow. You moving in is one of the best things that has happened in my life. You're like family to me. I love your children. And you're just as much a friend to me as Daisy. I know you'll move out once your divorce is final, that you'll date and fall in love, that Madison and Henry will head off to college. You all will go on with your lives without me, maybe forget about me, but know that I'll never, ever forget about you. You and your children brought light into what was the darkest moment of my life, and I'll never forget that."

Judge Beck stared at me, his expression unreadable. "Are you...are you drunk?"

Crap. Had that speech been so hokey that he thought I was drunk? "No. It's been three hours since I finished off my glass of wine. I'll admit that Daisy was a bit heavy on the pour, but I doubt I'm still buzzed three hours later."

The judge continued to stare at me a moment. "You're my best friend, Kay. I've known you less than six months, but you're my best friend. And I really needed that going through what I'm going through right now. I loved my wife, and this whole divorce has tossed me like a windstorm. Everything I thought I was working toward in life has been turned on its head. I have…I have to figure out what I want for my future, both involving the kids and myself. And I just don't trust anything I feel right now. But as crazy as things are right know, I know I can trust you. And I know you're my friend. You're my anchor, Kay. And my kids love you. You're their anchor, too."

My vision blurred and I looked down at my knitting.

"We'll never forget you, Kay." His voice was soft. "We'll never forget you. I'll never forget you."

It wasn't until I headed upstairs a few hours later that I realized the ghostly shadow in the corner of the room had vanished sometime that night and hadn't reappeared.

CHAPTER 19

I got up early in the morning and put together a coffee cake, shoving it in the oven and leaving a note for the judge and the kids before heading out to Marshall Heights. I'd intended on slipping the letter from the mortgage company with a note in his door and leaving, but I noticed the lights were on and I saw motion inside, so I knocked on the door.

It took a while for Melvin to answer. I heard the tap-tap of his walker, then the creak of the hinges. He smiled when he saw me and invited me in.

"I really can't stay," I told him. "I just wanted to give you this."

He took the letter and read it, his hands shaking as he reached the end. "What does this mean?"

"It means that a lawyer shouldn't need a huge retainer to present this to the county on your behalf and stay the eviction until the mortgage company completes their investigation. In fact, you might be able to file this yourself. Just go down to the courthouse on Monday and ask them what you should do."

He nodded, folding the paper and sliding it into his pocket. "Thank you. I don't want to get my hopes up too much but thank you."

"You should get your hopes up," I said. "Just promise me you won't ignore this. I know you're not well but take this down to the courthouse and say you want to appeal the eviction. Call me if you have any trouble and I'll get half the journalists in the state on it."

I didn't see where he'd have any problems. Spencer Thompson was dead, so there was no one to push for the eviction. It seemed Melvin Elmer would get his six months. And maybe even his house back for whoever might inherit his estate.

"Can I offer you some coffee?" he asked.

"No, I need to run. I've got a cross-country meet I'm going to go see this morning. Is there someone to help you out, though? Someone you can call on if you need something?"

He nodded. "My friend down the road, Ralph Stephens. He drives me places when I'm not up to it. He's got my fridge stocked with food. Checks in on me a couple of times a day. I'm okay. I don't need much. Lately I spend most of my time reading and napping and enjoying the last of the blooms."

Ralph Stephens. That name sounded oddly familiar. I looked out the big kitchen window into his back yard and felt a horrible suspicion crawl over me as I realized where I'd heard—or seen—that name recently. "Do you mind if I see your yard? Your gardens are lovely. I've been wanting to do something different at my house, and I love what you've done here."

"Of course." He beamed and led the way. I followed slowly behind the man and his walker, noting the oxygen tank sitting beside a comfy chair, a book draped over the arm.

"I have a mix of perennials and annuals," Mr. Elmer said once we were outside. "That dogwood was the first thing my wife and I planted when we bought this house back in 1962. The azaleas over there were put in soon after."

"Do you mind if I take a few pictures?" I asked him as I admired the huge azaleas.

"Go right ahead. You should come back in the spring when the lilies are in bloom. Or in June when the peonies are flowering. Although the lilacs are always my favorite. I open the kitchen window and can smell them clear through the house."

The gardens really were a work of art. I snapped pictures with my cell phone, then thanked him for allowing me to see it all. He beamed with pride, obviously happy to share his beloved plants with an admirer. It made me feel guilty for having such horrible suspicions. The man was ninety. He was clearly ill—so ill his neighbor had to drive him places and check on him several times a day. There was no way Mr. Elmer could have...well, done what I'd suspected. No way.

I drove back, feeling a bit ashamed at even entertaining such thoughts. When I got home, the judge and kids were already up and already digging into the coffee cake. We bundled into Judge Beck's car with chairs, blankets, a cooler for drinks, and enough snacks to survive a month in the wilderness. It was a wonderful day. Madison came in third and fifth in her events. I ate pizza with the judge and half a dozen excited, sweaty teenagers, then back home I barely had time to change before Daisy picked me up for our spa treatment.

I got the foils. And all my nails, both top and bottom, were a lovely shade of dusky rose when Daisy dropped me back off at home. She'd had the works in preparation for her date tonight with J.T. at Etienne's. I told her to have a great evening and headed into my house, a bit deflated that I had nowhere to go and no one to admire my lovely highlights and haircut tonight. Well, no one except for Taco.

All gussied up and nowhere to go. But instead of feeling sorry for myself, I cuddled my cat on the couch and made my way through a few chapters of one of the Luanne Trainor books. The main character, Trelanie, had just escaped yet another dungeon, this one filled with summoned demons, and in a surprisingly domestic scene was doing laundry, trying to remove demon guts from her favorite t-shirt while Roman watched, brooding and sexy as always even in a public laundromat in the middle of the night.

I had some laundry I needed to do, although there were no demon guts on my shirts, and no brooding vampire to watch me. Remembering the conversation with Daisy this morning, I tried to think of Matt Poffenberger leaning against the dryer, staring at me with the sort of hooded-eyed intensity that I always envisioned when I thought of the book's vampire hero. The image made me chuckle. Matt was a handsome man. He was kind and funny and dedicated to both his aged father and his charitable works. I closed my eyes and tried to think of some scenario where the two of us might have a romantic relationship. It was a little difficult with a purring cat on my lap and the shadowy ghost of my husband hovering at the edge of the couch, but I managed. The two of us at a romantic dinner. Walking together, his arm around my shoulder. Us in an embrace. Him kissing me.

The thoughts were...pleasant. I guess that was a start? Eli had been gone only six months, and the thoughts still felt like a betrayal, but Daisy was right. A second love might not be in the cards for me, but I at least had to be open to the idea that it might happen. And just like I'd reminded my friend many times, love doesn't always come with an instant rush of feeling, an explosion of fireworks from the very first glance. Some things took time. So I resolved that if Matt Poffenberger or some other reasonably attractive man, were to ask me on a date sometime next year, I'd at least consider saying yes.

A half hour later, Taco's purrs turned to meows and I realized it was dinner time. I dumped him on my porch for a few moments to chase bugs and roll in the flower beds, then went in to pour his Happy Cat into a bowl and pull the left-over stir fry and quinoa from the fridge for myself. After sticking my food in the microwave, I went out front to find the cat. Normally he was impatiently waiting on the front porch to come in and eat, but this evening he was across the street and a few doors down, bumping his head against Dora Tennison's leg. The woman was kneeling and looked to be dead-heading marigolds. I headed over to retrieve my cat, noticing that she was putting her clippings in a little basket, no doubt saving the seeds for next year.

"I'd expected you would have had something more exotic than marigolds out in this bed," I teased the woman as she rose to greet me.

"There's something about them I've always loved." She surveyed the flower bed fondly. "My mother always had them around her tomato plants. They have this astringent smell and are so easy to grow from seed each year. And they're so cheerful. Marigolds. The quintessential middle-class family's annual."

"And not poisonous?" I asked.

"No, although dogs and cats can get an upset tummy from eating them. You're not so foolish, are you, Taco?" She picked up my cat and gave him a quick scratch on the head before handing him to me.

"Happy Cat over marigolds any day," I laughed. "Actually, I wanted to ask your opinion on something. I'm not an expert at identifying anything beyond a few common flow-ers. I wondered if you'd look at some pictures I took of a garden and see if there are any of those toxic plants we discussed yesterday on my porch."

"Of course." She waited while I dug out my phone.

I handed the phone to Dora. "What do you think?"

She took it and enlarged the picture, scrolling it around on the screen and peering at the plants close up.

"Well, I think that's a lovely garden. Very English country in how it's organized and the types of plants they've chosen. And yes, I see both tall buttercup, although you might not recognize it without the blooms, and larkspur. Oh, and there's some delphinium as well tucked back in the corner there."

I nodded, taking the phone back. "But these are pretty common plants, right? It's not like only two people in the county would have tall buttercup, or delphinium, or larkspur in a back garden?"

"They're not the sort of thing most casual gardeners pick up at Lowe's or at the local nursery and garden center. And this garden isn't what I'd expect to see if a homeowner paid a local landscaping company to put one in. They usually go for readily available, commonly seen perennials and annuals like begonias and mums interspersed with hydrangeas and butterfly bushes. Maybe a row of impatiens and pansies along the front. Whoever put this garden together really knew their plants, and carefully chose what they were putting where for maximum effect. They did a wonderful job. A lot of care and thought went into that."

Melvin Elmer had lived there since the house was built. He was the only homeowner. And from what he'd told me, he took loving care of that garden himself.

He had motive—revenge. He had means right there in his back yard. And as for opportunity...I wondered if the receptionist at Fullbright and Mason would recognize him as one of the people who'd come in to see Spencer Thompson the day of his death? Without that, there was nothing to put him at the scene, and only circumstantial evidence tying him to the murder. If the toxicology report came back as tall buttercup, anyone could have gone out into a field and harvested some leaves—anyone who had a grudge against Spencer Thompson.

But would some random, angry person know enough from an internet search to get the level of toxin high enough to kill? From what I'd read, drying the leaves diluted their poisonous effect, as did heat, so someone would have needed to chop and grind them up into a paste and perhaps make a liquid coffee-like concoction to add to Spencer Thompson's drink.

"How well do you know the local hobbyist gardeners?" I asked Dora, stuffing my phone back into my pocket.

She shrugged. "Casual hobbyist? Not at all. If they came to a few of the seminars we put on at the county fair, then I might recognize them, or even know their name."

"How about someone who created and maintained that garden in the photo?"

She smiled. "She, or he, is probably a member of our horticultural society, probably a Master Gardener like I am. When you have a love of plants like that, you want to share that love with likeminded others."

An idea hit me. "Do you know Melvin Elmer?"

"Melvin Elmer?" She blinked in surprise. "Goodness, I thought he'd passed away decades ago. Yes, he was one of our Master Gardeners. Lovely man, but after his wife died about thirty years ago, he stopped attending meetings and became a bit of a recluse. I'd forgotten all about him. Very talented man. His wife, Ellen, used to come to our meetings with him, although he was the avid horticulturist of the family."

"Did Melvin Elmer know about the toxicity of plants? Enough to know how poisonous these alkaloids were, and what components and circumstances would create a fatal dose?"

"Well, of course. We've given annual seminars regarding toxic plants since I've been in our group. They attract quite the crowd—mainly people trying to ensure their dogs and cats don't accidently ingest something that might kill them. I do remember Melvin actually giving the seminar a few times. His wife used to joke that he could be a one-man bio-warfare unit. But you don't seriously think *Melvin* could have intentionally poisoned someone, do you? That man couldn't hurt a fly."

Unless that fly was evicting him from his house in the last six months of his life. Although, to be fair, I didn't see Melvin Elmer as a cold-blooded killer, either. He was such a nice man, but even nice people could do terrible things if pushed too far.

Still, none of this was proof. He had motive, and he had the means and the knowledge. But unless I could put him at the scene of the crime in a close enough window to have been able to cause Spencer Thompson's death, I couldn't go to Detective Keeler with this.

What if I was wrong? I didn't want to have a dying man spend the last six months of his life in jail because I'd jumped to conclusions.

CHAPTER 20

I mused on the situation for the rest of the weekend, wondering whether Melvin Elmer was really capable of murder or not and hoping on Monday I'd find out Detective Keeler had arrested someone else. Monday morning did bring an arrest, but for a different crime.

"Did you see this?" J.T. slid a copy of the local newspaper in front of me.

"Yes, I did." I was one of three people who still got actual newspapers delivered to their home each morning, even though I did tend to get most of my news online. There was something comforting about having a paper on my front lawn at six o'clock in the morning, having it spread out on the table as I drank my morning coffee, hearing the crinkle of the pages as I looked for the continuance of the front-page articles.

This morning's front-page article was about the arrest of a Michael Oak, who was an underwriter for Peabody Mortgage and had allegedly orchestrated a fraud scheme. A spokesperson for Peabody said they were in the process of determining which mortgages were fraudulently obtained and would be reaching out to homeowners (and former homeowners) with offers of restitution. They estimated the theft totaled approximately four million dollars.

"Seems your Mr. Elmer might be able to stay in his home after all."

My stomach twisted at J.T.'s words and I thought of the gardens outside of the man's kitchen window. Motive. Opportunity. Knowledge. Should I dig further and unearth what I was fearing? Or turn a blind eye and just let Detective Keeler handle this himself?

"Yes, he might, although I'm sure the mortgage company is talking financial restitution. I don't know if they can snatch back a home title once a place has been auctioned off and probably resold a second time after that."

But I was sure most people would be happy with the money. And as for Melvin Elmer, I doubted he'd find anyone pressing for an eviction, especially now that Spencer Thompson was dead. I couldn't see Marissa moving forward in the next six months, especially with herself a suspect, and having assets to track down as well as an unexpected funeral to arrange. I thought of the woman red-eyed at the coffee shop, telling me that she still loved her husband, and felt a wave of sorrow. Spencer Thompson had been a horrible man, but that didn't mean his wife wouldn't mourn his death.

"I want to know why this Michael Oak wasn't halfway to Mexico with his four million dollars," J.T. commented.

"Maybe he didn't have four million himself. If he had a partner, or partners, he could have only had a million of his own."

Only. I couldn't imagine having a million dollars, but I guess people got greedy when they began to steal, and suddenly a million wasn't enough.

I got to work on this week's skip traces, still trying to figure out if Melvin Elmer really had gotten his revenge on Spencer Thompson or not. It seemed implausible that an elderly dying man had prepared a poison, then driven to Milford to an office building to poison a man, then driven back home. But he hadn't been at his house when I'd dropped off the forms to temporarily stay his eviction. Where had he been? He looked frail, but it wasn't like he had to walk to Milford. Or climb three flights of stairs to reach the office. Elderly people got around, even with walkers and oxygen tanks. Had he driven there, signed in using his friend Ralph Stephens' name, and dumped poison in Spencer Thompson's coffee cup? Was his friend Ralph in on the murder? Was he the one who'd delivered the poison as Melvin waited in the car outside? Melvin wouldn't have known if killing Spencer Thompson would let him keep his house, but it certainly wouldn't be the first time someone was murdered for revenge.

And then there was Michael Oak. It couldn't be a coincidence that so many of the houses Spencer Thompson bought at auction were ones with Peabody Mortgage liens. And it seemed more than a coincidence that a man who was a victim of Michael Oak would find his house owned by Spencer Thompson.

Maybe I was looking in the wrong back yard for tall buttercup.

My phone rang, jolting me abruptly from my thoughts. A few seconds later I was gathering my things, with a quick excuse to J.T. and a promise to be back after lunch.

It had been Tracey Abramson calling, and he wanted to talk. It was odd how these four men were so intertwined in this mess—Melvin Elmer, Michael Oak, Spencer Thompson, and Tracey Abramson. I'd reluctantly ruled out Mr. Abramson as the killer after my talk with Detective Keeler, but in the back of my mind, I still wondered if he wasn't involved.

Hopefully I'd soon find out.

* * *

I SAT across from Tracey Abramson, comparing the swank country club restaurant with the coffee shop I usually frequented when meeting clients. Although Mr. Abramson wasn't exactly a client.

"I wanted to meet with you after our conversation the other day." The man flagged down a waiter and ordered coffee and a pastry basket for the two of us. As soon as the waiter left, he turned to me once more. "I didn't kill Spencer Thompson."

Well, that was getting right to the point. I decided to play along, even though Detective Keeler had convinced me that Mr. Abramson wasn't exactly a top suspect.

"You told me that you didn't like his business practices, that you feared his actions would damage the reputation of your foundation. You also told me that you'd been trying to dissolve the LLC but had been getting resistance from Thompson to do so."

"That's not enough of a reason to murder someone," Mr. Abramson insisted.

"No, but Thompson setting up a scheme where he skimmed half the profits from a property sale is. When you found out that Spencer owned Brockhurst Properties, the very company that had been the one buying Humble Properties, LLC homes at far below market value based on a bogus appraisal, then flipping them at closing to an actual buyer, that had to make you angry."

"Yes. It made me furious. And when I confronted Spencer at his office Thursday morning, it was to tell him we were done. I told him he was to sign off on dissolving the LLC immediately, or I would be contacting my lawyer. I held all the cards, Mrs. Carrera. There was no reason for me to kill him."

Tracey Abramson had been to see Spencer Thompson Thursday morning? Thompson had *really* had a bad day with three contentious conversations. And death. Yes, a really bad day. And it didn't escape my notice that Mr. Abramson's name hadn't been on the sign-in list that Detective Keeler had showed me. Was this what being a rich long-term client meant? No need to sign in? Just waltz right past the receptionist area and on down the hall.

How many other people had done the same? And I didn't remember showing any identification. How easy would it have been to go in under a false name, claiming to be there for a financial consult, only to slip some poison into that big, flashy coffee mug on Spencer's desk?

"If I had made any of that public, Spencer Thompson would have lost his job," Mr. Abramson continued. "Reputation is everything in the financial services world. Having a large client bring forth proof that he was skimming money off the top of business deals would have ended his career. He would have been blackballed."

"Maybe he wouldn't have cared." I shrugged, smiling in thanks at the waiter as he sat a coffee in front of me and a plate of muffins to the side. "Maybe Spencer Thompson was making so much money flipping homes under Brockhurst Properties that losing a job at Fullbright and Mason and having a black mark on his reputation wouldn't worry him a bit. A man with money to invest isn't going to get doors slammed in his face, no matter how unsavory his actions may have been."

A muscle twitched in Tracey Abramson's jaw and I knew I'd hit a nerve.

"Do I look like the sort of man who would drop cyanide into someone's coffee? I don't even know where to get cyanide, or any other poison, for that matter. I don't kill people, Mrs. Carrera. I pay my lawyer to bury them in expensive lawsuits. That's my weapon of choice."

Which was pretty much what Detective Keeler had said, and I believed him—both of them. "Why do you care what I think, Mr. Abramson? I'm not the police, I'm a small-town private investigator who spends her free time knitting, baking, petting her cat, and doing fundraising for local charities."

"Because although I'm one of the many people who didn't like Spencer Thompson, I'm one of the few people who was in his office, or cubicle, that day. And I'm one of even fewer people who saw him the day of his death and basically threatened him with legal action."

"More people threatened Spencer Thompson that day then you think," I commented wryly. "And as you said, your methods involve slamming someone with your lawyer, not poisoning their coffee. I'll definitely let the police know about our conversations if it comes up, but don't think you're at the top of my list of suspects."

He sat back and smiled in relief. "Good. It wouldn't do my reputation or my foundation any good to have me hauled in for questioning, or even brought up on murder charges."

Which was another reason I agreed with Detective Keeler that the murderer wasn't Tracey Abramson. He most likely didn't know anything about poisonous plants. He was assuming cyanide was the poison. It wasn't his style. And he was far too concerned about his reputation to do something so crass as murder. He had motive to want Spencer Thompson out of business, but not nearly the level of motive to resort to murder.

We finished our coffee, and I headed out, wishing Tracey

Abramson a good day. Then, with a significant amount of trepidation, I headed for the police station. Detective Keeler pushed a copy of the newspaper over to me as soon as I sat down.

"I saw that," I told him. "Is this your doing? The Peabody Mortgage arrest?"

"No, it seems a few of their title agencies were questioning their lien assertions, and internal investigation quickly revealed one of their underwriters was involved in fraud."

"You do realize that Spencer Thompson's Brockhurst Properties purchased six houses at Peabody Mortgage foreclosure sales? And that there is some question about where he got the initial funds to start his company?"

"You're implying that this Michael Oak was in league with Spencer Thompson?" Detective Keeler didn't sound all that surprised at the idea.

"That's exactly what I'm implying. A partnership gone bad? Maybe Spencer was feeling the heat and wanted to end their scheme? Maybe Oak was afraid Thompson would bolt and he'd be on the hook for everything?"

"He's already on the hook for everything, because Thompson is dead. Can't turn evidence on a dead man for a lesser charge now, can he?"

"Still, he could be the murderer," I insisted.

Detective Keeler smirked. "I do work on weekends, Mrs. Carrera. Michael Oak lives in a condo without access to even a potted begonia. The man can't tell a rose from a cabbage. He's not our killer. He did, however, confess that he met Spencer Thompson five years ago at a conference, and that Thompson would give him a list of names and Social Security numbers for elderly people in our county that would make good targets for Oak's fraud scheme in return for a cut of the deal."

"He still could be our killer," I said, desperate for it to be anyone but the man I suspected.

"No, he's not our killer. Now why are you here to see me on this fine Monday morning?"

I took a deep breath. "I know someone who had motive to want Spencer Thompson dead. He also has plants in his back yard that are poisonous and could kill someone in the manner that Spencer Thompson died."

"And," Detective Keeler prompted.

"And he's a ninety-year-old man who has six months to live and gets around with a walker and an oxygen tank."

The detective blinked. "That doesn't sound like someone physically capable of murder."

"He gets around just fine, only a little slower than most. He's a Master Gardener. He knows plants and he knows poisonous plants in particular. He's one of Michael Oak's fraud victims. He lost his house to foreclosure, and Spencer Thompson bought it at auction. The man was being evicted. He'd spoken to Spencer Thompson on the phone several times, begging him for a stay on the eviction, telling him that he wouldn't sue to get the house back if Thompson just let him live out the last six months of his life there."

"Was his name on the list of clients that Thompson saw? The list of visitors to the firm that day?"

I squirmed. "No, but the name on the list before mine, Ralph Stephens, is his neighbor and his friend. Maybe this Ralph is in on it, or maybe the man I'm thinking of used his name to get in."

"I confirmed the visit of every name on that list, so I doubt someone got in using a fake name. Ralph Stephens in particular has been a client of Fullbright and Mason for over a decade, and he wasn't even there to see Spencer Thompson."

"He still could have slipped something in Thompson's

coffee on his way to meet with a different advisor," I countered. "Or maybe his friend was with him and didn't sign in up front. Maybe he snuck in."

"The receptionist already admitted that every elderly man coming through the door looks the same to her. I doubt she could pick one over the other in a line up. But still, I'm pretty sure she would have noticed someone hobbling by with a walker and an oxygen tank."

"He doesn't always need the oxygen tank," I protested. "And maybe he doesn't always need the walker. He's the only suspect with motive, opportunity, and the knowledge to kill Spencer Thompson. And you already said the receptionist probably wouldn't notice one additional elderly man heading through the office doors."

"What sort of poisonous plant do you think this man used?"

"Tall buttercup and/or larkspur or delphinium. They're both highly toxic alkaloids according to my expert, and the manner of death from ingesting a concentrated dose is consistent with the way you said Spencer Thompson died."

"Buttercup? Like the stuff that's in every median and field in the county? You're seriously expecting me to haul a ninety-year-old dying man in here because he's got buttercups in his back yard? What's next, arresting people because they've got dandelions in their grass?"

"Not just any old buttercup," I protested. "Tall buttercup. Some buttercups are more toxic than others. That particular variety is very toxic. It blisters on touch. Swallowing it would lead to severe blistering of the mucus membranes and gastrointestinal tract. Swelling of the throat and airways due to the reaction. Asphyxiations. And if that didn't kill them, the bloody diarrhea probably would."

"A lovely image just before lunch, Mrs. Carrera," Detective Keeler drawled. "Imagine for just one moment what would happen if I arrested an elderly, terminally ill man who had been the victim of identity theft and fraud and accused him of murder just because he was one of the hundred people who would have motive to see Spencer Thompson dead, and just happened to have some lovely flowers in his back yard. Imagine what the local newspaper journalists would do to me. I'd be a viral Twitter sensation by the end of the week. I'd have people sending me hate mail and writing nasty things on my car. My boss would pull me into his office and yell at me. And the prosecutor, because she's a smart woman, would absolutely refuse to bring charges against the man."

"But if the toxicology report comes back that the cause of death was larkspur or tall buttercup—"

"It's still not enough for me to commit career suicide by accusing a ninety-year-old dying crime victim of murder. You get a picture of this man standing over Spencer Thompson's coffee cup, pouring a vial of something into it, and we'll talk. Actually, make sure that picture is time and date stamped, and then we'll talk."

I walked out of the police station, a bit humiliated, a bit frustrated, and, I'll admit, more than a bit relieved. Was Melvin Elmer the murderer? Just because the facts were pointing his way didn't mean he was guilty of murder. And even if he was, did I really blame him?

CHAPTER 21

"*T*hank you. This looks wonderful." Melvin Elmer beamed at me and sat the espresso-chip pound cake on his kitchen table. "Can I offer you anything? Coffee? Tea?"

"No, thank you. I just came by to see how you were doing and if there was anything I could help you with. Anything I can pick up at the courthouse for you? Groceries?"

That wasn't why I was there, but if Mr. Elmer did need something, I'd be happy to help him out.

"I actually just got back from the courthouse. Took your advice and went in to see about getting that eviction canceled. And I spoke with a very nice lawyer on First Street that said she could help me with the house title for a very reasonable fee. I might actually come out a bit ahead after the mortgage company settles."

"That's wonderful news. Guess you'll be unpacking then?"

He nodded. "My friend Ralph from down the street is coming over later to help. Luckily I don't have much to unpack."

I glanced out the huge kitchen window into his back

yard, admiring the daisies swaying in the early fall breeze. "Mr. Elmer, there's something I have to ask you. Where were you Thursday around twelve-thirty when I came by to drop off those papers from the courthouse?"

"Hmm?" He looked at me with raised brows, then smiled slightly as he glanced out the window. "Oh, I had some errands to do. A few financial matters to take care of. The bank, things like that."

"Your friend Ralph drove you?"

"Yes, he did. He had a few errands of his own to run as well."

"So the two of you didn't go to Fullbright and Mason?"

Mr. Elmer shrugged. "I really don't know. Ralph had a quick meeting, and I waited in the car. It was a nice day and I get worn out walking."

"You didn't go in with him to confront Spencer Thompson?"

"No, of course not. Why would I do that? He made it quite clear over the phone that he wouldn't hold off on the eviction."

"Perhaps you thought that if he were dead, he wouldn't be able to evict you?"

His smile turned tolerant. "The eviction had already been granted by the court. His death wouldn't have stopped it. And who's to say there wasn't an heir or other owners at Brockhurst Properties who would continue on with the eviction even after that man's death?"

"Then maybe you wanted revenge," I pressed. "Tall buttercup. Larkspur. It wouldn't have been too difficult for someone who knows their flowering plants. You made the poison, and your friend Ralph dumped it in Spencer Thompson's coffee."

"Goodness, that would be quite the friend, poisoning someone for me while I rested in the car. I'm sure if you were

174

to speak to Ralph, he'd tell you how ridiculous an idea that is."

"There are a lot of things people will do for their best friend," I told him. "And murder for revenge isn't all that ridiculous an idea."

"Would you kill for your best friend, Mrs. Carrera?"

I hesitated, wondering about the answer to that. My initial impulse was to deliver a vehement "no", but I knew in my heart there might be circumstances where I put my morals aside. If someone hurt Daisy or Judge Beck, I'd want to see them in jail, but if someone were to hurt Madison or Henry…. Yes, I most certainly was capable of murder if the circumstances justified it.

Mr. Elmer sighed and leaned against the kitchen counter, suddenly appearing every bit of ninety years old. "I wasn't interested in revenge, Mrs. Carrera. All I want is to stay here in the comfort of my home, and hopefully live long enough to see my lilacs once more."

It was clear I wasn't going to get a confession out of the man, and I wasn't exactly sad about it. What the heck would I have done if he'd confessed? Watch them haul him to jail? I was so conflicted about this whole thing, but I couldn't see taking any more of this man's time.

"You're looking a bit tired," I said. "I'll let myself out. You've got my number. Please call if you need anything."

He nodded. "Thank you again for the pound cake. I'll definitely enjoy it. I'm sure Ralph will too, if I decide to let him have a piece."

I headed for the door, hesitating as I heard him call my name.

"Mrs. Carrera?"

I turned to see him standing in front of the kitchen window, haloed by the afternoon sun behind him.

"I'm not someone who would kill for revenge, but I'm *glad*

that man is dead, because now he can no longer harm help-less people." He nodded. "Or people he *assumes* are helpless. No one else will ever lose their home because of that horrible man. In my eyes, justice has been served."

* * *

"YOUR HAIR LOOKS NICE," Judge Beck told me.

I reached up a hand to pat the slightly blonder locks that I'd attempted to style in the same way the lady at the spa had. The judge and I were home alone this Monday night, the kids having gone to their mother's for her week of custody. That usually meant late nights for the judge and lots of dinners alone for me, but tonight he'd breezed through the door promptly at six o'clock, bringing take-out lasagna from a new place across from the courthouse. I appreciated the dinner. And I especially appreciated the compliment.

"Thank you. I might make this spa day a regular thing."

"You should." He reached over to gather up my plate. "Did you bring home work for tonight, or dare I suggest a movie?"

Oh, definitely a movie! And ice cream!

"I've got a few skip traces I was going to work on, but they can wait for tomorrow," I said.

"All done with your divorce case and the hidden assets?" He started rinsing the dishes and I watched. A man doing housework had to be one of the sexiest things ever.

"All done, although I feel like there were a lot of loose ends." I sighed. "Loose ends don't make me happy. I'm sure her lawyer will find the other banking accounts, but I don't know if we'll ever know how complicit Spencer Thompson was in those mortgage frauds or prosecute his murderer."

Judge Beck turned to eye me over his shoulder. "Prosecute? So you have your suspicions?"

"I do, but it's very circumstantial. I told Detective Keeler

176

everything I knew, put it in his lap, and he said that unless I found the proverbial smoking gun, he wasn't going to proceed. I know this man did it. In a roundabout way, he hinted that he did it. But it's not enough to send him to jail."

"Do you think this man will kill again?"

"No. In fact, I'm positive he won't."

"Then sometimes you have to be satisfied that someday, somehow justice will eventually be done, Kay," Judge Beck told me.

But what really *was* the definition of justice in this case? Even with a smoking gun, Melvin Elmer would be dead before they brought him to trial. Even if he lived long enough to stand trial and was convicted, he'd not live long enough to serve out his sentence. Would his punishment be not seeing the spring blooms and lilacs one last time? Somehow that punishment seemed more severe than the crime warranted. A man's life had been taken, but that man had been a thief that had cost at least six people their homes, had stolen from his partner, and had cruelly denied a man the dignity of dying in his home. I wasn't sure that meant he deserved to die, but I didn't see where causing Mr. Elmer more pain than he'd already suffered would be the right thing to do.

Besides, I didn't have any hard proof that he'd actually done it. Or that his friend Ralph Stephens had been involved —either knowingly or not.

Last week Judge Beck had told me that sometimes a person had to be happy with partial justice. That's what this was. Partial justice. I'd done all I could, and those whose responsibility it was to find and arrest a murderer had declined to act. I guess I had to be satisfied with that. Partial justice. And maybe somewhere down the line, there would be another judge to play King Solomon. Maybe that judge would be Saint Peter at the pearly gates. And if so, part of me hoped he opened those gates wide and let Mr. Elmer inside.

"Chocolate or vanilla?" I asked the judge as he loaded the rinsed plates into the dishwasher.

He shot me a boyish grin that made my heartbeat pick up a notch. "Why choose? Let's have both. And I'll even let you pick the movie tonight."

ACKNOWLEDGMENTS

Special thanks to Lyndsey Lewellen for cover design and typography, and to both Erin Zarro and Jennifer Cosham for copyediting.

ABOUT THE AUTHOR

Libby Howard lives in a little house in the woods with her sons and two exuberant bloodhounds. She occasionally knits, occasionally bakes, and occasionally manages to do a load of laundry. Most of her writing is done in a bar where she can combine work with people-watching, a decent micro-brew, and a plate of Old Bay wings.

For more information:
libbyhowardbooks.com/

ALSO BY LIBBY HOWARD

CPSIA information can be obtained
at www.ICGtesting.com
Printed in the USA
LVHW050800130121
676354LV00005B/518

9 781733 069151